THE MAYOR OF
NEW ORLEANS

THE MAYOR OF NEW ORLEANS

JUST TALKING JAZZ

by

Fatima Shaik

CREATIVE ARTS BOOK COMPANY, BERKELEY
1987

For information contact:
Creative Arts Book Company
833 Bancroft Way
Berkeley, California 94710

Typography: QuadraType, San Francisco
Cover Design: Charles Fuhrman Design

Library of Congress Cataloging-in-Publication Data

Shaik, Fatima, 1952–

THE MAYOR OF NEW ORLEANS

Contents: The Mayor of New Orleans • Climbing Monkey Hill • Before Echo.

1. Louisiana—Fiction.   I. Title.
PS3569.H316M39   1987   813´.54   87-71147
ISBN 0-88739-050-1

Printed in the United States of America.

Table of Contents

When I look upon the waterfall
And feel that every drop has known some land
Whose captured harmonies must now expand
In bursts of praise that rock the spirit's wall,

I think the Lord made poets of us all.
What matter if in tongue, or eye, or hand?
The spirit yields but to His own command
When sudden light and love and grace enthrall.

—Lily LaSalle Shaik
April 14, 1948

THE MAYOR OF NEW ORLEANS

JUST TALKING JAZZ

"YOU MIGHT THINK I'M SIMPLE," SAID WALTER Watson Lameir, "but they ain't nothing black or white."

He had reached the beginning, his crescendo of story, with the young man who walked into Buster Holmes' restaurant at Burgundy and Orleans streets. It had taken Walter a few beers to get the visitor into a listening mood, primed as they say on the farm, oiled as the hookers might repeat who worked in the classy districts around St. Charles Avenue.

Walter knew a man needed preparation for stories. Up the Mississippi River in Garyville, Louisiana, where Walter claimed to grow up, people might commence over a piece of sugarcane. It took a lot of jawboning by listeners and participants before the tale was sucked sweet and the husk dry.

"Shoot. I'm in New Orleans, Louisiana, the U.S., the world. Ain't nothing simple about that. Looking at me, you might could imagine you know all about me," Walter was coming to an arpeggio, the bridge. It would be repeated and resounded until the audience cheered. Walter, besides being a storyteller, was a musician, "his true heart," as he might say. He was a Dixieland trumpet player, a Coltrane saxophone imitator, an appreciator of Mangione, and a "mayor of New Orleans," he told the young man. "You, son, are looking at the former mayor of New Orleans. Now don't go and asking me none of that political stuff, like legislation, jurisdiction. I say like I want to say. Politics is of the people. And I am of the people. That's why the people elected me."

1

Walter looked at the visitor, a sorry little young man, as people go. Jack, he said, was his name, Walter believed. Looked like his mama had slipped a too big T-shirt over him and stuck his legs through baggy white shorts. If he tucked in his shirttail, Walter knew, he'd be wearing elastic waist.

"Well, ain't you sick and tired, Jack," Walter continued, "of them officials in starchy white shirts, neckties strung up so tight they face look like blood on the banquette." Walter pointed to the sidewalk to indicate the place he meant.

"You tell him, Yonar," a patron called from the back of the bar.

Walter continued, "Those fancy politicians, they cross they legs at the knees, how a friend of mine Jim used to call it, they push they thighs so tight together, they squeeze all their good juices up to they brains."

"Hot dog," the bartender hollered, testifying like church.

The clients hooted.

"Far shore," exclaimed a man alongside Walter who had been listening. He wore a cowboy hat scrolled tightly on each side.

"Look out," the bartender called again, nodding his chin to the side in the direction of the cowboy.

The men at the bar cackled some more.

But Walter looked a little disappointed, which is hard for a man like him. He was too tall, too healthy a physical being to look downtrodden. His chest was broad, although its focus was slightly lowered. His arms still showed ripples even though they were now under a layer of fat. Walter had the wide rubbery face of a man who knew what to do with his mouth when the situation demanded it. He was the kind of presence that people like Jack in their hometowns of New York City and Detroit would either cross the street to pass or else ignore.

Walter took some offense that his story had been interrupted and he looked down into his draft Dixie beer. The bubbles separated themselves like the past, present, and future. Some settled under the foam, some dissolved into the air.

Still, it was Jack's flimsy and insular-cultured self that Walter wanted to address. People like Jack believed too little, especially about people like Walter. His sensation sometimes about this circumstance was akin to madness.

"Look, little brother," Walter leaned over to Jack who was rocking slightly from alcohol, "it is obvious this your first time in New Orleans; let me take you aside. Let's go for a ride in a carriage. I got a friend. I will tell you how I got to be the mayor of New Orleans and show you the best reasons for why you came here."

The men left the bar, stepping through the screen door into an ice white sun. They reduced the clientele in half when they left. But patronage was always forthcoming at Buster's. A plate meal could be eaten for less than a dollar. Everyone did his part to entertain for free and educations were doled out with as little as possible pain.

Walter and Jack headed for a step across the street on the corner. "So we catch my friend when he ride by, if in either direction," Walter pointed out. The cement was hot. But there were two wide natural seats where the banister would have been. Giant steps framed each side of the little pyramid stairs up to the door.

Walter sat on the top level with his feet on the second level. Jack, on the left, did the same.

"The sun ain't too much for you, is it, boy?"

Jack shook his head no. The heat was sobering him, making the big, black man next to him appear frightening.

Walter said, "You not ready to go, huh? Listen.

"How many time you vote in your life?" Walter asked Jack as they sipped the ice water that Walter had returned to Buster's to get. Walter guessed that Jack was in his mid-twenties, but pretty sheltered. So Walter had given Jack an opportunity to leave if he got too afraid.

"I suppose about three times," Jack replied. "Only in presidential elections." Walter figured he got Jack's age about right.

"I never did vote until I was old as you. But that's because I couldn't. At least I used to did tell myself. Come integration and all that, and voting rights, and I could have march and things. But I never did it.

"Nothing, nothing in this world mattered more to me than playing my horn. I used to wake up the people next door to me. Lord, when I was a boy, they used to complain. And I lived in the country. I came to New Orleans when I was eighteen.

"I was happy as a queen on Bourbon Street. Don't need to look around afraid like that, Jack. In New Orleans they don't mind the publicity. I been to some of their balls around Mardi Gras. Shoot, they have the best time around town."

Jack started wondering again what he had gotten into. New Orleans was such a strange place. In other cities, people were against each other or for each other so violently. But never unless there was some vested interest.

Here, he thought, life arranged itself so incongruously. The vines grew out of the bricks. He saw them in the back of his hotel. Some flowers coming into his windows and lizards crawling into his room.

The cleaning lady told him, "Won't harm you. They'll eat the cockroaches. Just let them be. They got no business with you and you got no business with them."

The streets here wound in circles and the names changed depending whether he was walking in the French Quarter or across Canal, over on the business district side. Jack wondered whether they changed the streets just for the tourists. But then he saw all those eighteenth century signs.

"This is the alley where the pirate Jean Lafitte killed most of his victims," the guide said when Jack joined a group to walk around. "And here are the slave quarters, aren't they beautiful? Some of our finest and richest people have darling quaint apartments there now. For two-fifty more, you can get another tour that will take you inside."

Walter tapped Jack on the shoulder, "I guess you be wondering how I got to be mayor. I'm getting around to it. Was because of unemployment. But first here comes my friend."

"Say, Edward," Walter called, "make some room in there for me and this young man from out of town. Where you going at? To water your mule? We just hop in and ride for a while and wait until you begin again."

The mule stopped in the middle of the intersection. It was tired of the foolish ways Edward drove. It was the mule's intention to embarrass the people. But the cars following it waited quietly and patiently until the men stepped up.

"Ain't this the coolest outside place in the city? Up here under the shade brim with the breeze coming through. You have to learn to love the simple things, Jack. That's what I learned from all my jobs," Walter said.

"But what about unemployment? . . . ," Jack asked.

"Whoa," said Edward, "don't be telling no sad stories in my cab. If you want to tell sadness, go cry in your bed."

"Nah, man. This is about my life. It is entirely glad," said Walter.

The mule listened too because it could not tell the difference between sadness and mirth and it wanted to know. The mule put its ears back against its head, as far as they could go with that flowered straw hat. People were always trying to dress up the mule like a lady. Genderless, opinionated but without any reason, the mule was not quite sure whether it liked that.

The men drove slowly to the trough alongside Jackson Square. Edward out of habit and pride pointed to buildings along the way. "That's the museum of voodoo, where they got Marie Laveau in wax and also the monster Lagniappe."

"Man, they must have took Lagniappe out of there years ago," Walter said. "I remember when I brought my kids. Had to buy them some ice cream they got so scared. And then me trying to explain to them what *lagniappe* meant when we were children, going to the store and getting a little bit extra than what you paid for."

"You the fool," said Edward, "I think your kids well understood that."

Jack asked, "Longyap is such a funny name. Is it Spanish or French?"

"I don't rightly know. Do you, Mr. Ed?" Walter asked.

"I think it got something to do with the revolution or pirates or something. Anyway, it's a real word. They always use it in the *Times-Picayune*," said Edward. The mule didn't read the daily newspaper. So it just looked all around.

"In New Orleans, isn't anything as it seems. Which brings me back to this truth I want to impress upon you, about my life," added Walter.

"I got to be mayor of New Orleans because I wasn't interested in nothing but music. Let me take you back."

"When I come here, there was many more gigs in the city. People didn't have Victrolas, except the rich. But on the

summer evenings there was music all over. Just on my block—
picture this—opera coming out of the long French doors like
bouquets of roses. Piano like good-time girls if you sat on the
step. Man and trumpet, that was my baby, coming sweet clean
at you from a window like a woman's lips, wet and delicious,
wishing with her heart you would give her a kiss.

"I was right in there. I'd go over to Jackie's and we'd talk-like
with music. And then sometimes Earl would come over, after
his job on the waterfront. If Delesepps could get away from
his beer and his wife after his day of painting houses, he'd break
out his violin. Man, you couldn't get a more beautiful situation
that that.

"Those were nights. And the days were like heaven too because no matter where you were you carried a song. Your feet
walked it. Your ears put the sound of the streets into it. Shoveling gravel, shoveling gravel, carhorn, carhorn."

Jack smiled at Walter, maybe this wasn't going to be so bad
after all. The mule came to an abrupt stop. Cars slammed on
brakes and drivers hollered out behind them. Edward gave them
a calm wave of his arm to pass by. Walter continued.

"And we made money. Because nobody, like I told you,
bought records. Come Saturday night, they'd hire us as the
band. House parties. Baby. You can't believe, liquor made in
the tub out of sugarcane. Dancing. Some of those girls like to
come out of Africa. They did their shoulders, they hips. Make a
man cry.

"Morning, somebody fix grits for breakfast and we go to
church. That's how a person stayed purified."

Walter had begun sweating. He took out a rag, which at one
time could have been a handkerchief, and wiped it tightly across
his forehead and neck. "Jack, do you believe me?" he looked up
into the young man's spellbound face. "I knew you would on
that part." There was a glossiness in the older man's eyes.

"People believe in our souls," Walter's wife had told him
when things started to become rough, "so we must." She reminded him that no one gave them anything that they didn't
work for or deserve. "So, baby, the truth is to trust," she said.

Times had gotten harder when the sweet music and life were
passed on to the youth. Like the children that multiplied out of

this union, hundreds of them all playing instruments, having contracts and managers, there was more music than parties, more parties than jobs. The days became tough. Such began Walter's search.

"So I began taking my music out to the streets," Walter waved his arm across the narrow French Quarter street caves. "Walter, Your Man in a Moment, my sign said," he laughed. "But nobody was looking for fast jive."

Walter remembered some part of this to himself. There was much to be done educating Jack, but personal had its points. There was a scene at his uncle's house when Walter was out of work that still pained him. His folks were his life and they felt the same way. But hunger put the devil in the best.

"Music has had its time and so has you," his uncle, Fredrick, had said, hard on gin. Walter's aunt, T'Ma, said, "We got plenty to feed anybody who comes to our table." She said it to defend Walter but she would not go as far as against her husband. But she made the money then anyway. She took in sewing for rich people. Walter wished he could play like that lady stitched, tiny threads close next to each other with bare swellings for knots near the buttonholes, big, firm even strokes around the hem.

The rich ladies never came over to fit. So T'Ma carried the clothes uptown. Until she left the neighborhood, she walked with the package sitting on her head. She'd bring back a French bread, quartee rice, quartee beans—each a quarter's worth—from the Italian grocery around the block. Then she'd cook it up so good you would never know meat wasn't in it.

T'Ma passed away so skinny that it hardly took men to carry her wooden box. Walter always thought it would have been better, although crazy if he had suggested it, if women balanced her coffin to the grave on their heads.

She didn't go much after that big argument in their house, Walter remembered. So he followed not far behind. He took his trumpet, and a little lace and a scapular with the bleeding heart of Jesus on one end and Mary on the other. He carried the smaller things next to a few dollars that he enclosed in a hand-sized piece of leather tied with a string.

Lots of his buddies were on "skids" as they called it back

then. He never knew why it was referred to as that, nobody got to slide. Nothing was smooth about those days, nothing rode. Still there was laughter and sharing and music. This was New Orleans; no pain was let to last longer than a tide.

"Sheet. 'Mama,' I tell her, 'this is New Orleans. You better get up off some of that cash.'" Sweet Percy was in rare form when he discussed his women, called himself a rider. He said, "Like the insurance man."

Percy was one of the few men, if you could call him that, Walter remembered, who made money when everyone else's things went bad. He gave them all entertainment for free. "That's all that's free around here," he reminded the men. He appreciated their laughter at his evil side.

Sweet Percy, Herbert Latousse, and Sam Miligan, "the Milkman," they called him because he was so white. Might have been real white, Walter remembered, but he acted so awful, who was to know or to care.

All the men joined at a bar on Rampart Street in the early morning. Walter learned to stop over there to see if any of the houses needed someone to play. "We got players and playees plenty," Walter was told by Sweet Percy, eating a big breakfast. He said, "My first meal of the day." Walter just laughed rather than hitting him. Times were hard.

Lavergne was a beautiful, sweet, generous woman. It pained Walter to think about her out in this sun. She was from south Louisiana, skin colored sunset like a peach and just as juicy inside. Lavergne made some of the best money for Sweet Percy, gave Walter some and sent the rest to her mother. "I do this because God gave me something to use to help others," she would tell Walter. He never knew whether she meant her customers, her mother, or him.

"This is New Orleans," Edward was saying to Jack. "It's a part of Louisiana, the South, the U.S., America, and the world. Ain't nothing different about it what goes on here, no. Just like anyplace else. But it's all the way different because all goes together when it happens here."

"How can that be?" Jack was laughing.

"It's funny. It's funny, you right. Ain't nobody to argue that with you," Edward went on.

"Like this here mule, beast of burden. But would you burden yourself with a mule? Before I goes home every day, I take and brush it. I waters it, feeds it—sweet hay and maybe a little molasses. I takes off that hat and straighten it out. Make it pretty for tomorrow. Then I make sure its bed all straight since it got nobody to sleep with. Then I goes home to my wife. What she tell me? I smell like a mule. I say, 'you look like a mule.' Then we could get on with dinner and I could play with my kids. I'm up early in the morning before my mule wakes up to take care of this animal here."

Jack was leaning back laughing. He was sipping a Dixie out of the can. Edward had reached into the cooler that he kept next to the horse trough and gotten them all cold beers.

"But it's the truth, I tell you," he was laughing also now and Walter had returned to the present and joined in. "Don't make me tell you again," Edward was standing in the front seat and addressing Walter and Jack as if they were children. They laughed. "If I tell you again, I might tell it different."

"And it still be the truth," Walter toasted Edward in the front and then Jack at his side.

"I'll tell you what is the truth. Columbus discovered America," Walter laughed.

"No. No. I got better than that," Edward added. "This is a genuine antique, miss. I give it to you for three dollars."

"How about . . . This Mississippi River water is the purest in the United States of America. Drink up," Walter said.

"Good girls don't kiss and tell," shouted Jack.

A moment of silence.

"Where you from, boy," Edward asked.

"Why? Uh. New York."

"Not in that shirt," said Walter.

"Well, really, just outside the City. In Connecticut."

"You ever had a good girl?" asked Walter.

"I guess," Jack said, "I don't know."

"Well, now you getting close to the truth.

"The only difference between yellows, browns, blacks, reds and whites is colored skin," said Walter, "And that ends it there, 'cause all them women got it and it runs all over them, covering them up.

"A woman will tell you the truth as she knows it and believes it and wants to think about it. That is the goodness of a woman and the foolishness of a man."

Edward leaned over his seat in the front looking intently at both of them, "My woman is as sweet as the rain in her heart. Her head, that's another story. And her behind, hot mamacita."

"Music and love is both women and truth is too. But what women ain't is politics. Women don't sleep with everybody just for a dollar. Not even the whores. They put some of their souls on the line," Walter concluded.

"You're going to tell me about when you were the mayor," Jack prompted Walter.

"I'm getting to that."

It was two in the afternoon, the sun blazed like a spotlight on the story Walter was about to tell. The men left the mule alone so they could go and get sandwiches "in the air condition." They entered a room that had the smell of oyster shells and the feel of sawdust underfoot. A waitress came up to them.

"Look here, baby. I want a hot sausage po-boy and, what you want, Walter?"

"Just a half loaf dress shrimp."

Jack looked at them both. "Do you have an American cheese sandwich and a salad?"

"I think we could find it," the waitress said and continued writing as the older men smiled.

"Women," Walter said, "they just full of truth.

"So, okay. I was out of a job, right? My woman, she say to me, 'Lameir,' she call me by my last name to get serious, 'What we would do if I have a child?'

"'Honey, don't account on that,' I tell her, 'I ain't got no job.'"

Walter explained he got a woman because times were so hard, he "could at least afford to have love.

"It was excellent. But more than anything, it was mine. Something I owned. I worked it and I deserved it.

"But love is a funny thing. There is lots in the world, all around. But you got to pick it out, like one of those wishes, you know those little cotton puff flowers that float around in the spring. You got to see it in the air, then chase it, then catch it. No matter if you look like a fool.

"The thing I had to learn was you got to hold it in your hand for a minute to make your wish, then you let it go. Even the children know that. But people get more stupid as they grow," Walter said.

"Now don't go getting ignorant, fool, just because we're talking about love. Ain't there is a sentimental in every man in New Orleans? I swear," Edward said.

Jack was about to ask if that was a question. But Edward shook his head the width of the bar to the air. No.

"What this Romeo is trying to say is that his Juliet left him," Edward continued.

"Went with a heartless man to the North," Walter said. "What could I do if she was pregnant? We had no money. I couldn't be happy. How I was going to support my boy, if it happened?"

"First of all," Edward said, "you don't know if it was a boy. Then you don't know if she was pregnant. Next, you ain't really sure she just didn't want to go North anyway. Case closed."

"Man, you want me to hurt you?" Walter stood up. "You give me some better words."

"Look, Lameir. Your second wife is with you now. She loves you. I love you. You my brother. Don't be moaning over no common-law gal. Besides, you told me yourself, she never could cook," Edward said.

"Man, she soak a pot of beans until you get sprouts," Walter smiled, "or either you find one of those rocks in your dinner. You swear you eating some of Laplace."

Jack chuckled, "Where's La Place? Is that a real place?"

"Man, real, what we trying to tell you, young son, is relative," said Walter.

"Relative, that's right," added Edward. "Like your first wife, your second wife, hope to God you don't get no third wife. That poor woman you got now if you don't start treating her better I'll trade in her for my mule. And maybe your mama too."

"Your mama, fool. What, she eat ignorant beans when she was carrying you?" Walter said as the beers arrived.

"So here I is . . . ," Walter was describing his past. The men leaned over their beers, their sandwiches gone to reveal only the white waxy paper they were served on covered with juice, a mixture of tomato catsup and mayonnaise. They looked into each others eyes, were attentive and teasing, and gave themselves over to the afternoon. "So I is here in the city then, with no first wife no more . . ."

"Done flew the coop," added Edward.

". . . out of work for a long time, if you call musicianing work, meaning only you get money. My sign, now, Walter in a Moment, people seen so much they think I'm stupid . . ."

"Well, there's some truth to that," Edward said.

". . . so like I say, I take to the streets.

"The streets of New Orleans are beautiful things," Walter continued. "You notice, Jack, how on some they laid in brick. Hand by hand, somebody's daddy did that, maybe their mama for all I know. But it was a person, a people thing, not like this here what they got—running over the tar squishing it to all sides like some skunk you done ran over in your car. Anyhow, on some streets, they got brick. On some they got gravel, uptown. Some of them streets out in the seventh ward, London Avenue for instance, was nothing but oyster shells, grey white with a pearl finish if you look at it on the right day, in the right frame of mind. But it smell; Lord have mercy.

"I know about all of these streets because I walked down every one of them. Carrying my trumpet in my hand, had sold the case. My scapular and my lace in my wallet, if you could call it that. And praying, baby, I prayed every day, sometimes twice.

"They were building Corpus Christi Church, putting up that nice stucco on the side, like Mexican style. Of course it was for the colored, how people was called in those days. The missionary priest and sisters came to New Orleans just like they went up to the Indian reservations in the north. One day I think I'm going to meet a real Indian and I'll be able to ask him, 'You ever have a run-in with Mother Ignatius? She box your ears?' I think that's half the reason I can't hear so good out of one side right now."

"Man, you know you hear what you want to hear. Don't talk about the nuns. The nuns kept you from being illiterate," said Edward.

"That's the truth, I'm not going to deny it. I'm not going to deny prayer either. As I was going to tell you before I was rudely, and I mean rudely, interrupted. I prayed like hell and I walked like them put on they shoes angels, 'all over God's heaven,' well, over earth. And come to be that a lot of people start recognizing me. "'Hey Walter,' they be hollering, 'hey baby, how's it go?' "'No dice,' I sorry to tell them all the time. But the people, they give me hope. They concern. 'Honey, I'd get my husband to put you on, if you knew how to do bricklaying work,' one lady tells me. "'Miss, I'd do anything,' I tell her. And she knows I'm telling the truth because she smiles. I won't never forget that pretty blush smile. But her husband tells me, times is hard and he got to hire his relatives and you know how many relatives they got in the seventh ward, count all the way to cousins fifth and sixth and cousins by way of living next door."

"So look, tell this poor boy what happened. He's getting older front of my very eyes," said Edward.

"I'm okay," said Jack.

"See, now. He's starting to get the hang of how we do things down in New Orleans," said Walter. He called the waitress for another round for the group.

"So I ain't walking the streets just to walk the streets, you know. I ain't no beggar," said Walter.

"Not unless you got the money to pay for that round you just ordered," said Edward.

"Not to worry. If I ain't got it, Jack got it. Right Jack? And we'll move around the corner where I know people for some more beer," Walter said.

"Sure," Jack told Edward.

"The reason I'm walking the streets," said Walter, "is because I am a musician. And you seen those jazz funerals where they march, right, Jack?"

"Sure," he said.

"Well, I was parading. I was parading myself from the seventh ward to the ninth ward, from Treme to the second ward. Back of the garden district to St. Roche cemetery. I was going to play me some music to get the people happy enough to give me money."

"Did it work?" asked Jack.

"Kinda. But you got to listen to my songs. First, I start off with 'Just a Closer Walk With Thee,' just like at the funerals. The people feel sorry for me and they think of all they old dead folk and how they wish they could hear that song. So they start singing along to themselves, you know, so the dead can read their minds. Then I do 'God Bless the Child,' like I learned in them roly-poly joints. The old ladies get sort of hushed on this one, like they're going to go away. But they know they stood outside of those places, at the farthest, and they like that music same as everyone. Then, 'His Eye's on the Sparrow . . . So I Know He's Watching Me.' They hooked then, they don't know whether to stay or go. You know, like the Lord caught them red-handed."

"Man, do we must hear all this?" Edward asked.

"You drink up, partner," Walter said. "Anyhow, I end with 'Way Down Yonder in New Orleans' and they begin to second line. Always got a few of the loose ones will shake their behinds and pass the hat for me."

"So you made out all right, then?" Jack asked.

"Well, not with money, with popularity," answered Walter.

"I think you going to be very popular here too," said Edward. "Here come the waitress to ask for your autograph."

"You got two dollars, Jack?" Walter asked.

"Sure," Jack put a five on the table.

Walter laughed, "Don't go show yourself, unless you ready to share."

They stepped through one half of the swinging door and it banged back and forth, slamming against the lip of the other and squeaking.

"I used to could make my music off of stuff like that," Walter said.

Edward called, "I got to go check on my mule."

"We with you," Walter responded.

They had not left the French Quarter but Jack felt transported. He was thrown to a time that he never lived. It was comfortable sometimes. Then he would feel totally out of place. He did not know these men. Both were old enough to be his father, or maybe his grandfather. He was not a good judge of black men's ages.

Although race wasn't the issue either. He had gotten over that back at Buster Holmes' when he decided to stay on the step. It was like he was handed some test of manhood by Walter. At the time, Jack thought, "Well, who is he anyway?" But he was glad he had waited. For himself, even, he felt that he had passed.

Why did they look at him so strange when he said, "Good girls don't tell" or "do tell," which was it? Anyway, didn't they think he knew women at all? He had been screwing since he was fifteen. Betsy Crinoline let him have it. She, he smiled, was very good.

"So you think I don't know anything about loving women, huh?" Jack caught up to Walter as he stood reading the weekly newspaper's headlines through the tin-enclosed stands while he waited for Edward.

"I got no problem with you and women," said Walter, "but you are wrong if you think you know about love."

He went on, "Who knows about love? Christ Jesus was the only one I heard of who I could say put the finger on it. It's just like truth. Mother Mary was the only one who knew perfect truth, never sinned. And then, what was done unto them, was that the truth or was that a lie? Was it love that killed him or hate? Did she and Joseph like each other or just suffer the presence of the Holy Ghost? Are we reading the Bible or is it some story people made up along the way?"

Jack's head was swimming with beer and with symbolism. "What does this have to do with women?"

"You say you know love. You think it's women. I say it is music."

"Walter, you bending this man's head," Edward approached them. "Why don't you let him come up for air? Anyhow, you supposed to be telling him when you was the mayor of New Orleans."

"Edward, where's your mule?" Walter asked.

Edward looked down at the ground and said weakly, "I think it's sick from the heat. I went over there and it's foaming a little around the mouth. I couldn't tell. And it ain't saying a word to me."

"You talking to it now?" Walter asked.

"Don't make me out no fool," Edward said. "You know how I rapport with that mule. Lay one side of the rein on his back, that mean turn to the left. Sing 'Watermelon, red to the rind,' it turn to the right. Most of the time I don't need to tell it the way home. I sleep from the French Quarter all the way to the stables. It stop at the lights and everything."

"Man, I just got a few beers in me. I'm sorry. I don't mean to make fun. So what you going to do?" Walter asked.

"Well, I figure I sit with it for a while, see if it get worse. I already put a little water 'cross his neck and sponged the back."

Walter pointed to Ursuline Street. "We just going around the corner. You know my place. Jack here ain't never heard music like what they got there. I want him to know."

"I hope your mule feels better, Edward," Jack said.

"Thank you, boy. I do appreciate to hear that."

The young man and the old man walked slowly from the horse trough to the cathedral. The ironwork fence around Jackson Square ran alongside them. It was upright like bars and open to show children playing games freely inside, the bums sleeping under the shade trees, and pigeons circling in packs.

Painters set up small easels every two or three feet. They brought ice chests and seat cushions along with their paints. People decided who was serious by what subject they chose to paint. There were caricaturists at the bottom of the list, then portrait artists in charcoal, then near the top of the list were the ones who did French Quarter scenes. Of course, people discounted the artists who just took little butter knives to apply oil paint from the tubes to raise the lines of a print that had been pressed in by machine. You could get them for far less money than the others, except the caricature people. So the knife people were the most popular.

"Wait, stop here a minute," Jack halted Walter by the arm. "I want to go into this postcard shop."

Walter waited outside next to the Mammy in a red-checkered dress with an apron and her head tied. She was stuffed cotton, like a big rag doll or something a taxortionist, he thought they called them, would do. People from out of town took their pictures with it. Children lifted the woman's dress to see if she had on underwear, or her scarf to see if she had hair.

Walter could imagine he lived in the old times of those Mammy laws, even though they were at least a hundred years before. His grandmother repeated the stories to him when he was a child: "They made it so we had to tie up our heads, all the colored women. It was against the law to show hair. They was afraid of our beauty. Had so many black, yellow, red ones having white men. They was as much afraid of our power, too, that we would put the love of white into our colored children. See, they wanted to keep pure their race."

As a boy, Walter had not believed her. But then later, he read the law in a book. His grandmother had been one of the greatest reasons he took up trumpet. "Play it loud so I can hear it from both ears," she said. She was a little deaf. She never seemed to notice when there were mistakes.

"Here, I bought you a postcard," Jack exited carrying a small brown paper bag. It was of a scene in Preservation Hall of old men playing Dixieland and Sweet Emma on piano. They looked sort of waxy and unreal, Walter thought. But he appreciated Jack's gift.

"You all right," he patted the young man on the shoulder. Jack was leaning up against a building and writing out a postcard against the old stucco wall. His handwriting was bumpy and scribbled. "This is for my girlfriend in New York." He handed the card to Walter when he finished it. It said, "Music is love. Jack."

"You going to be an old sentimental yourself, as Edward say," Walter told Jack and patted him on the shoulder a little harder than before. "Come on, let's get around this corner a minute. You make me wonder what I'm talking for."

Walter had seen so many young men come and go in New Orleans. Visitors, he was thinking about. Not that they had to be white. He remembered a young man he befriended from New York, said he was a writer. He wore a watch chain across his stomach, which was pretty wide. It went from one pocket in his vest to another. He wore the vest over a white T-shirt. Edward didn't want to pick him up. He told Walter that was some kind of sign.

"Well, I was the fool to make a friend with him," Walter told himself. That time, he remembered, it hurt. Walter saw his life's story in a newspaper someone brought back from New York, except the man had written it into fiction without even mentioning Walter's name. He wrote in the paper that he had a vision of the South in his head, although he preferred to live in the North.

"I'm a friend to every man," Walter remembered his conversation with Lapin at the bar where they were going. "Ain't it true that I reap what I sow?"

"True. You reap friendship, not fame, Walter. But maybe that's not enough. Look at you now, you got no place to go," Lapin said.

This friend had encouraged him to run for mayor. "You out of a job anyway. What can you lose?" Lapin was called that since he was a child because of his buckteeth in the front and later for the quick staccato style that he blew clarinet.

Walter got into the mayor's race more for Lapin than anyone, at least anyone he could name. He felt for Lapin, being made fun of all his life. Lapin was a most excellent musician. But because of his funny looks, he never was given serious fame. The others Walter ran for were the people. He knew that sounded crazy when he told it to his wife.

"You some kind of revolutionary? Walter, you not on LSD or something you picked up in the French Quarter, are you, baby?" she said. He explained he was doing it for her, for her friends, and for the beauty of life.

"I knowed when I married you, I married a sweet man. That's one of the reasons I love you," she had said. "God bless us, baby, for what we about to do. But why not?'

Walter went back to Lapin the next day to tell him to begin the campaign. Lapin said, "What? You already got one."

They put flags all around the bar and crepe-paper ribbons outside that washed color onto the building with the first good rain. People who had been saying, "Hi, Walter," when he walked around town with his trumpet and sign came to the bar to have a beer, hear him talk and play.

Walter felt his message then. He blew for the lady with the "rag round her head," he told the people, who lived on the corner of London and Rocheblave where she hung up the wash. "Washwoman Blues Monday," he told the audience that the song was called. It sounded like the call of a goose. His music was like that, sort of funny, sort of pitiful. Everyone who came there could relate to that.

From the bandstand, Walter could see big men wiping their eyes in the dark, and ladies and children who came during the day were singing along.

He did "Washwoman," "Schoolteacher's Vacation," and "Garbageman's Strike." The last song he was inspired to create during the police boycott of Mardi Gras. When the television cameras asked a garbageman if his union would go out in support of the police, the man said, "Them what you go to support today be the same ones who tomorrow beat you in the head."

Walter himself had gotten swung at a few times. When he was a teenager, he and Lapin went to the parades. Lapin jumped up to catch some beads and came down accidentally on a woman's foot. Even though he apologized, the woman screamed and screamed. Walter tried to reason with her, "Miss, you can have one of my doubloons. Don't be upset on Mardi Gras." But she was from out of town.

The police came at them swinging. Walter and Lapin got struck a few times. But they were able to run. "Just remember, what you don't say when a cop got a stick at your head," Walter told the crowd to prepare them for the music, "is 'please, mister don't hit me.'"

The audience laughed.

Walter's memories, sometimes he felt, were like waves. Like out on Lake Pontchartrain where he sat on the seawall steps. First you could sit on the fourth step up from the water, then the sixth up and soon you had to sit up at the top. The water in the evening would be coming, rolling, splashing, never really announcing that it could do you real pain. But if you were fool enough, Walter remembered, like Bootsie, to stay planted on the step in defiance, the waves could sweep you off and take you away.

"Bootsie, that was a fool," Walter smiled, "a man who would try damn near anything and see if he live." Most of the time, like that evening at the lake, his friends loved him so much because of his foolhardiness, they would save him. Walter himself, not much of a swimmer compared to the other guys, had also jumped in.

"But didn't we have a time?" Bootsie asked Walter once after they got older and Bootsie worked in a wrecking yard. They leaned up against a hollowed-out car. Bootsie said, "Man, I loved ya'll brothers for that so hard."

"Sheet, you a fool, Bootsie," Walter had tried to make it into a joke. But after, he thought maybe it was the wrong time. Bootsie's wife left him not too long after that and Bootsie committed suicide.

Jack told Walter, "You got awfully quiet. Is something wrong?"

"Shoot, not no more than I'm thirsty and somebody better be buying the next round."

"Not me," Jack said, trying to joke as he had heard the men do before.

"How you know?" Walter asked him.

"Well, uh."

"Jack," Walter started laughing, "You got a lot yet to learn. Come on in."

Walter escorted Jack by the shoulders alongside him up to the bar. "Lapin, where you is at?" Walter called. "I want service from your hands."

"Wait, man," Lapin called, "I got to go to the bathroom . . ."

"Isn't that thoughtful," Jack said, "for him to go wash his hands?"

". . . I ain't dirty enough." Of course, Lapin didn't go to the bathroom. He came directly over to them at the bar. "My friend," he said to Walter, going to hold palms and shake.

"Your mama," Walter said, shaking his hand.

Jack was getting dizzy, not understanding what was real. Who was good? Who was bad? He looked up, north to the sky, for assistance. Then he saw one of Walter's campaign posters. "Is this some kind of joke?" he asked the men.

"You know, Lapin," Walter said, looking at Jack, "You tell people the truth and they don't believe you. They want to think the worse about you. But never that you could be something."

"I'm sorry," Jack said, "I'm not trying to be offensive. It's just so . . ."

"A joke, man," Walter said, "It's a motherfucking joke and so am I. That's what you think?"

Jack reached for his beer. What had he done? This man was trying to be nice to him. He apologized again. "I'm sorry, Walter. I'm from New York. Things don't happen like this up there," he said.

Walter responded, "You'd be surprised."

"Now, Connecticut . . ." Walter said, "I would believe anything about Connecticut. Ain't that is where they got the New Haven slums and Yale? Remember Laurent went up there after St. Augustine High School when Yale came recruiting. Went to Africa and then became a Communist, as I remember. Ain't that right, Lapin?"

"Yes, but he is a peaceful man and he still go to church," said Lapin.

"Well, he want to be buried by Corpus Christi Parish and you know how they strict," said Walter.

"I'm sorry, Walter. I am from Connecticut," Jack looked down over Walter's beer.

"Look, young man, don't get all worried about that," Walter said. "Just don't bullshit me. There's a lot of truth going on here."

"You know what's the truth?" Lapin called out to both of them. "That fat women taste like candy kisses."

The men laughed.

"I swear," Lapin sang. "Look at my own sweet wife." He handed to Jack a black-and-white photo that was stuck in the cracks between the frame of a mirror behind the bar and the glass. "You might not think she is a lot to look at," Lapin said to Jack, "but she is as good as a summer day is long. And the nights," Lapin gazed into the air, "thank God they so short. I'm getting kind of old to keep that load lifted for hours."

"For hours, sheet," said Walter, "not for that long in many years, Lapin. But me, like the song says, 'I'm the sixty minute man.'"

"Music," Lapin reminisced, "Music is what brought me and my sweet lady together." He looked at Jack, "You ever been to hear James Brown?

"Well, let me tell you," Lapin continued, "here, every year, they used to have a James Brown concert at the municipal auditorium. The auditorium, you know, is back of Congo Square. That's the place outside, where when in slavery, they used to bring the slaves on Sunday and the people would have parties and socializing. That, they say, dancing and socializing, is the difference in the slaves of the English and the French.

"Anyhow, about this time as I was a young man, I'm talking about twenty-five, thirty years old. Walter here is older than me. I used to go every year, hear James Brown. He wasn't so popular those days. At least not with all the people buying his records, like now. Then they put his face on the cover and, anybody know in those days, wasn't nothing but us going to look at us on the cover of albums. Not even Johnny Mathis, they didn't put him on for a long time. But anyhow, in person, JB, Lord, he put on a show.

"Well, the white people never came to those concerts either. Because people be partying so hard, they about to kill each other to death. Always was one humbug or another there. But nobody except the troublemakers really get hurt."

Jack watched in amazement. Lapin seemed to have forgotten he was telling the story to him. Lapin looked out over the bar into the air as he talked or sometimes he would direct his conversation to Walter.

"Anyway. One night at the JB concert there was a shooting. Bam. Bam. Bam. People started flying down the aisles and out the door. Me, I ain't no fool either. I go running straight to the St. Bernard bus. But guess who I'm following behind?"

"Your wife?" asked Jack.

"You right, young man. There she was barefoot as she want to be, running with one shoe in her hand. She jump on the bus and sitting there either between laughing or looking foolish, she telling everybody who could hear that she left her good shoe under the seat in the balcony. Well, I liked her way about life. We got to talking after that."

"Lapin, that is a love story if I ever heard one. You ought to go get somebody to write it up in one of those magazines," said Walter. "I don't see why the *Times-Picayune* wouldn't publish it in the 'Lagniappe' section, the lagniappe being ya'll got married besides being in love."

Lapin looked at Walter, "You know that's a thought."

The sun felt like it was still high. It might have been four or five in the afternoon. But no one was going to go outside to look up and see. There were no clocks in the bar. "That's bad for business," Lapin told Jack. None of the men wore watches. Jack, because he didn't want his stolen in a strange city. Walter and Lapin, because in their words, "our time is our own."

"Still, now, you ain't heard me out about being the mayor. You know, I don't believe you want to know?" Walter swiveled his chair to face Jack.

"No. That's not true, Walter," Jack apologized.

"I'm just playing with you, boy," Walter responded. "We're all over that."

Lapin prompted Walter, "Tell him about the time we had the big parade. Started and ended right here at this very bar."

"OK," Walter said and leaned over to Jack, "do you know the difference between marriage and death?"

Before Jack could answer, if he could answer, he was so busily searching his mind, "Participation," said Walter, "that's the truth. This is how I want to tell you about that parade."

"Once," he began, "once a man marries, he has full knowledge of what he is doing. Oh, him and a few women, they been around. And his kin, they so happy, he's joining them under the wedded yoke. They come to the church as if something was free. And it is. And then they dance at your reception.

"Man, if you never been to a Creole reception. How long you be here? I should take you. There is so much dancing and drinking, rival any house party or whorehouse. But there is not a bit of evil on anybody's mind. Not big evil, at least. Maybe some venial sins, like your sister get soused and call her mother-in-law a name or maybe everybody dividing up who going to dance with the single girl and one of the men break the group and ask her all alone.

"Well, marriage is like that. Joy, drinking, dancing. Then you may ask, 'Then what, I do not see it, is the difference with death.' True, then all the same things go on. And all of your family takes part as well, bringing their sins with them. Except there are other guests.

"Some people who come to your funeral be glad to see you is

dead. Others come because they are still with the living and they misses you as one of their number. They don't know you either. But Lord, do they cry. Well, that's what I'm getting at," Walter said. "The difference between marriage and death is the same as political parades."

"I don't understand," said Jack.

"It's the same people what do all of these things. For the same reasons. Except quicker. They love you or hate you and dance with you, for you or against you all in a few months' time," Walter concluded.

Lapin showed Jack mementos on the walls of the bar. There was a sign saying, "Walter, the Candidate for the Moment." Stuck in the mirror were photos of Walter with the president of the United States, a lady with a fruit basket on her head, and a child dressed up in an outfit like a ham. On the costume was a blue ribbon; it said First Prize. "That was a lawyer friend of mine daughter," Walter said quietly. "They too had they hard times."

"We used to have lots of his literature in here," Lapin said, "but I had this waitress once who used all the flyers for bar napkins because we ran out. Can you imagine? I had to let her go the next day. Some people don't have no appreciation or respect."

"Must have been every musician in town came to that parade. The old ones who come dragging they feet and the young ones who played nothing that hadn't been electrified. They all came to strut, like I said, for all their different reasons. But Lord, that was a day. We covered some ground," said Walter.

"We started right here at Lapin's bar. Everybody got the first round free. He's such a good man. Then we took to the street. We went down to Buster's to pick up some people, over to Esplanade and up to Simon Boulevard. He was a war hero, you know. Go look at the statue. We went over to Charity Hospital, stood out there and played for the sick for a spell. Then we came up the back, right to City Hall.

"They got a big spot full of grass in front of the mayor's office, you know. So we played and we played. Some women I knowed in grammar school, who were then secretaries, took our literature and went pass it around inside."

Jack could picture this. He knew lots of secretaries. He saw women in suits and high heels, knocking on every door in the tall City Hall building and giving each office worker a pep talk.

"Shoot, that girl Irene went home and got her slippers." Walter reminisced. "She said she was going to walk around City Hall plaza for me all day.

"But it was the sound that got me over, I know. Everybody playing his own tune then coming together at the bridge like that. You heard what they call Dixieland music, huh Jack?" Walter asked.

"Yeah, I studied it once. It's A-A-B, A-A-B," he said.

"Well, you could say that," Walter patted Lapin's arm. He was always impatient. "But it's more like, listen, 'Let's go around, ba-rump-bump. In low down, ba-rump-bump. Old New Orleans, ba-bump, ba-bump, ba-bump ba-bump bump.' You could do a big lot of shaking on that." Walter saw from the corner of his eye Lapin was now smiling and humming along to himself.

"Well, that's what the people did. They shook they behinds so bad, they made up they minds to vote for me. Lots of people. You couldn't count how many yourself. They checked those machines on election day for three times. Nobody could believe I got the votes. The politicians said, 'How this fool done come in here with no power, no organization, no people backing him and win, come to be the mayor.' I say to them, 'Fellas and some of ya'll who is ladies too, that's where you wrong. I got people who always wave to me when I go down the street. I got power 'cause power is people. And I got organs and organization, the head connected to the neck bone, the neck bone connected to the shoulder bone, the shoulder bone connected to the chest bone, the chest bone connected to the . . . well, you know that song, don't you Jack?

"Anyway," said Walter, "that's how I come to become mayor. But a man is not a job. So that's not my story. That's just the half of it."

"I was no more or less a man as the mayor than as the unemployed," Walter told Jack.

"Is this a morality tale?" Jack said, a little drunk, showing his youth.

"Ain't no tale at all. This is the truth," Walter answered. He was drunk by this time also and did not understand the offense, as it was slight.

"The difference between where I was before and then," Walter said, "was words. I still had the heart of a musician. I still had my natural gift of gab. But because they named me the mayor, people looked at me in a different way."

Edward walked into the bar. "How's it going?" Lapin greeted him.

"Man, I'm messed up," he replied.

"What are you angry about?" Walter asked.

"My mule ain't sick. Not really. Somebody just went and gave it some ice cream. All of that white round his lips. The mule got milk and sugar drying up all over his face. Drinking water to get the sweet taste out of his mouth. I tell you people are crazy," Edward said. "A mule ain't a child. If they didn't have nothing to do with they ice cream, why did they buy it? Now I'm going to waste a whole evening working because that animal is nauseous. But you know I think I saw him smile?"

"Give the mule some peace," Walter patted a chair for Edward to sit down. "Come trouble us. We used to your kind."

"Walter was just telling Jack the difference between a job and a man," Lapin called out.

"Well me myself," said Edward, "sometimes I would like to know that."

"Remember when I was the mayor?" Walter asked Edward, "remember what happened then?"

"All kind of people want to come up and shake his hand, ask him his personal business, make him pronounce how the black people felt," Edward turned to Jack.

"Well, at any time, anybody can tell you I be glad to talk about all of that," Walter said, "but it was because I was the mayor they asked me. Not because I was Walter. It was like that children's story, remember that fairy tale about the boy who couldn't take off his hat.

"They be asking me this and that. Not 'cause they had no respect for me. But because they wanted to hear the mayor's words. And if I tell them, they laugh, meaning to hurt in a way because that's not what they expected from the job," Walter was interrupted.

"You know what the black man's burden is, Walter?" Lapin asked. "It's that he speaks the things that people don't believe. They can't or don't want to believe or something. I ain't figured that part out yet. But I know it's the truth."

"You right, my friend. I could tell you from firsthand experience," Walter said, "remember I was the mayor and lots of folks couldn't even listen to me. Oh, it was all right to them to vote for me as long as I was a musician. But being the mayor, by their own rules, deserved respect. And couldn't many— black or white—give that to a black man—mayor, musician, or what."

Walter remembered he'd had to get bodyguards for his wife because she shunned some men in the grocery store. She never was the kind of woman to play along with men. But after he got elected, people said she was trying to act stuck up.

"Who is the mayor's wife now?" Walter remembered the newspaper headline. She was who she always had been. But now, men were calling at her, reporters following her down the street, women studying her hair and wanting to hear her speak. But she just wasn't the kind of person to give her opinion. At least, not to the public. Just to Walter, he smiled, just to Walter.

"Having a job was hard as not having a job," Walter remembered to himself, "and it was all on account of words." Not only was he named new and people had a particular suit for him to fit, but they started dragging for him about the way he used English and what books did he read and why did he attend the Catholic church.

At that time, Lapin did Walter the favor of going to the library and bringing back some books for him. "Look here," Lapin handed him a novel, "I thought this one would be interesting. It's by a man-woman, James Joyce. I don't think that name is totally for real. But the lady at the library said it had a lot to do about speaking in different ways. He's from Ireland and you like them."

"Yeah," Walter had said, "my great-grandfather was from Ireland, Conden. So I got no problem there. That guy Milkman we used to know, I think he was Irish too. But he was kind of rough. Then look at his company, Sweet Percy. So I guess all peoples is about the same."

Walter still remembered the story he had read about the girl who was going to marry a sailor. It reminded him so much of his little cousin. Except his little cousin took the boat and left New Orleans with the man. She had so many in her family to support. Went to Miami and came back home without him, rich.

But Walter remembered, he did learn something from those books. Everybody talked as bad as him. Some of them might try to act more proper or like they owned the English language. But the books showed that people put words together all kinds of ways, just like music. And Walter knew about music; in music, there was no such thing as more right.

A man could play a horn sweeter, Walter remembered, like Miles. Or a woman could sing worse sad, like Billie Holiday, queen of the blues. But to say that an aria, Walter knew opera too, was better than a riff, only a true fool would presume.

Outside the evening was falling like a cheap window shade, the best buy for the people who loved summer because it still let the breeze and some light in too. It gave a blue mood to an old-fashioned room. On one side of the big double doors, the grandmother would be kneeling in the reverent half-brightness and saying the radio rosary. On the other side, by the round lion-footed table, the mother would be setting out plates.

The evening smelled like onion smothering down into brown gravy, if you strolled on your way home past windows in the seventh ward. The voices of children playing would surround you like music. And in fact, many times, they would be singing. "Miss Mary died. Oh, how did she die? Well she died like this. One, two, three, four. Miss Mary died. Oh, how did she die? Well she died like this. One, two, three, four." The little girls would be following the leader in the middle, holding their backs or their sides or their chests, in repetition. "Well, she died with a heart attack in her sleep. Never coming back to live on this street." Then they'd pick a new leader. "Miss Sarah died. Oh, how did she die. Well she died like this." The new child might spin her forefinger around her ear to show Sarah died of insanity.

Each child would go inside, some before darkness fell, some much after, as their people called them.

"I was not a happy politician," Walter told Jack.

Jack was looking out of the open door to the street. It was beginning to get dark. He felt, for no reason he could put into words, like he wanted to run away.

"Man," Edward called Walter, "are you buying beer for people or what?"

"What." Walter said, "Could you put one of those cold ones out for me. I'll take care for Edward with you tomorrow."

"I know where you live," Lapin said, "not to worry."

"I was happiest," Walter said, "most entirely happy playing music. There is nothing more pure than sound alone."

"Think about it," Walter put his hand on Jack's shoulder. Jack jumped just a little, coming out of his personal thoughts— subways, money, getting a cab from the airport.

"Listen to what I'm telling you. If you are by yourself sometimes in the middle of the night, you can hear the earth spinning," Walter confided.

"Oh no. There goes crazah," Edward called. "Man slow down a little bit on those beers."

"Don't pay no attention to him," Walter leaned back to Jack. "I got an idea *why* you can hear it. It's a proven fact that you can. Ain't that the truth, Lapin?"

"Well, man, I ain't never listened to it with you. And you say you can't hear it unless you alone. And me, I got a house full of children," Lapin replied. "But I ain't going to argue with you about it. Stranger things done been proved."

"Well then, all of ya'll listen. The earth, you see, she is like a big, twenty-five-cent gumball. You know, like those jawbreakers we used to buy when we were kids . . ."

"You talking about the day-old donuts from Dequoux?" Edward asked.

"No, not them kind of jawbreakers," Walter said, "the kind you used to suck on, the hot ones, like you used to put in a handkerchief and try to crack with your teeth if you was in a rush, you know. You'd have all the little pieces in your handkerchief and you'd sneak to eat them bit by bit during class."

"I know what you talking about," said Lapin, "the children who used to study a lot would just suck on them real slow until they melted to a tiny round ball of sweet in the middle."

"That's the jawbreakers I'm talking about," Walter said. "Well, big like that in comparison to a circle that you would draw in the dirt to play chinees. Ya'll might have called it marbles, Jack, where you was a boy. I know that's just New Orleans.

"Well, imagine a big blue jawbreaker sitting in a circle of chinees, everybody staring at it, wondering what it's doing there? who's playing with that? will it stick to the ground? Just then a bully comes by, picks it up, and throws it farther than can anybody see. And this being a special blue jawbreaker, it just keeps flying, humming out into the air. Scooting away forever. That's the universe.

"And then what would all the children say? There would be so much commotion, laughing, fussing, teasing. Maybe even some of them who really wanted to find out about the jawbreaker's reasons for being there would cry. But I can tell you, wouldn't it be loud then?"

"Most assuredly," said Edward.

"I hear you," said Lapin.

"I've been in a situation like that before," said Jack.

"Yes, it would be loud," Walter went on. "Now imagine yourself, you a little bitty tiny ant. In size, less than an ant . . ."

"A uncle," Edward joked.

"Shh," said Lapin.

"So you this little living speck, on this big jawbreaker. And you stuck on it. So when the bully throws it, you go too, flying faster than you could ever imagine in the air. What does it sound like, children hollering, you flying, the wind all around you whistling by? It sounds like the earth spins. I don't need to see it to know it's a fact.

"I am not a visual person," Walter said. "I once had a college woman tell me that. She must have been right. Said she learned in school, some people are visual and some people go by what they hear."

"Aw, that's a story," said Edward.

"No, for real," Walter said. "Like Edward here," he told Jack, "he is visual. Me, I listen for things. But Edward, he could tell you what things looks like all over New Orleans."

"Well, that's the truth," said Edward. "What you want to know?"

"How does the city look during Mardi Gras?" asked Jack.

"Huh, you asking for a lot of seeing," said Edward, "get me another beer."

He began, "At Mardi Gras, you know that's a religious holiday, all over the city, the people are colored. Got on red suits, bright blue dresses, dirty brown baby diapers, wearing big green palm trees on their heads. And I'm just talking about the grown men.

"The woman, they are the most beautiful, drunk as they want to be, too. But some of them put on they sexiest clothes, bikinis, backless evening gowns. Some of them dress like nuns.

"It's the spirit that makes everything look different then. That, plus they mask. In New Orleans, if you masquerade you can really come out with yourself. But don't let people recognize you. They'll holler, 'I know you Mardi Gras.' Then you been found out."

"Tell him about the Indians," Walter encouraged.

"You ever seen a black Indian?" Edward asked.

"Well, I guess," Jack said, "like some of you have Indian blood, right?"

"No, I'm not talking race Indian. I mean real Indian, like for Mardi Gras. The Wild Magnolias or Wild Tchoupitoulas. Some named after the uptown streets. That's where lot of them were born.

"When I was a boy, you'd wake up early on Mardi Gras to go see the fights. The uptown Indians would fight with the Indians that lived below Canal Street. My mother said don't get mixed up with all of that. But I went," said Edward.

"Us too," Walter spoke for himself and Lapin.

"You could know they was coming if you look on the street and see the flag boy arriving up front. The scout probably passed already but you missed him. It was his job to be sneaky and spot them who they was going to beat up on. Then he'd go back and tell the chief.

"By noon, they be so full of firewater, the most they could do is just give out a few bloody cuts. So that's when they had the good times. Be in a circle on the neutral ground, you know, the grass dividing the uptown from the downtown sides of the traffic. And second-lining. The best.

"Now, talk about looking pretty. They costumes was full of beads making pictures, yellow like a egg sunnyside or black like a good racing horse. Every bead, the warriors sew on themselves by hand. And I think they really be wishing not to get into no fights to get all covered up with blood."

"Edward," Walter interrupted, "was you ever an Indian?"

"I was for a few months until Mardi Gras," Edward said. "Then my mama catch me going out of the house and stole my clothes. They laugh about that too hard on the block. So I decided none of them really was my friend worth giving up my life."

Edward continued, "But the saddest thing I ever saw was a Indian burial. Much like the shouting Baptists, some of them anyway. There was screaming and falling out on the ground. A little girl, about fifteen, she was this warrior's lady. He was the same age. She went up to the hole and threw his costume in. I thought she was going to go in herself. But I think she wind up having a baby. Then going back to high school."

"I never heard that or even read about it in the guidebooks before I came to New Orleans," said Jack. "I thought I covered everything."

"Might never would 'cause it's our story and that's about history, man," Walter said. "Lapin knows all about history."

"Man, you trying to tell me I'm old or something," Lapin joked.

"You could be old as you want to be," Walter said. "I know you remember and you read."

"Don't be spreading that around, man. I'll lose my reputation as a good bartender . . ." Lapin leaned toward the group to do his part for Jack.

"History, she's a funny thing, Jack," Lapin said directly to him. "Each person has one and everybody has one. So can't never anyone agree on it."

"Yeah, like that time you say that wasn't no vision that they had on Laharpe Street," Edward said. "Look Jack, it was the Blessed Virgin Mary appeared in the bathroom. I seen it myself. At least what she left. There was a little shadow right next to the tub in her image and likeness. Just like her."

"Well, man, you know how I feel about that," said Lapin. "The Blessed Virgin Mary don't need to go to no bathroom. She give her vision to other places, where people need her. Like in Mexico, remember how she did them roses in Guadalupe," said Lapin.

"I don't know about no Guadalupe. I'm talking about Laharpe Street."

Walter stopped Edward, "Let the man talk."

"We'll settle this later," Edward said.

"See, like everyone knows history. But they know it in a certain way. And ain't none of it true. Then again all of it is. It's like America. The things you learn in school go up against the things you know from the street. Like, they say in New Orleans, the Spanish did the ironwork balconies. But I know for a fact that one of my people was the best ironworker in town. And he was pure de black.

"But then black is not a real people color anyway. It's not a race, it's a political term. . . ."

"I'm going to finish telling you to about my political term, Jack," said Walter.

"Yes," said Lapin, "he definitely got to hear about that. I'm just going to be another minute . . . black neither white is nobody's skin color. You ever seen it?"

"Maybe some of the African people?" said Jack.

"Not to be offensive," said Lapin, "But hell no. Even them, they ain't black. They might be purple-brown, or oil-mud color. But never just black. Ain't nobody white. They might be egg-shell or ivory or milk-cream. So why do they call all of us that?

"Because of history. Because somebody wanted to read everything in a certain way. First, they have the war, the revolution of immigrants. Then they got to make they own history and system. So they decide to make it in a black-and-white way. When the first American people choose to take on that name, they have to make a thing out of their race. Is you white? Is you black? Is you other? We is all other—Italian-Chinese, German-Cherokee, Haitian-Irish, ain't that what you is, Walter?"

"Just on my grandmother's side. I got French, Spanish, two or three Africans and Indians, and some other stuff," he said.

"See, that is history and that is his right," Lapin concluded.

"But I don't quite understand," Jack said. "You are saying that there are racial differences. But you don't want to call it that."

"Of course, everybody is different. That's what I'm saying makes them the same. That's what makes real history. Everything told in between black and white," Lapin answered.

"So what does a person believe? How does a country unite itself?"

Edward spoke up, "I don't see where nothing is falling apart. It's about the same as it always was, in my life. Except now, some is trying to make you think we wrong unless we all think the same thing 'cause we stuck together by land north and south."

"Look out now," said Walter. "Out of the mouths of fools."

"I be reading the paper too, man," said Edward.

"I know it, baby," Walter replied.

"What a person has to believe," Lapin said, "is the truth. That's what you have faith and trust in. And the truth can come from any side."

"Now ya'll ready," said Walter, "this here has to do with why I am not the mayor no more today.

"They ain't room for the truth in mayoring," said Walter. "Not like music playing or basketball or swimming."

"Man, remember how we used to go swimming at Lake Pontchartrain before it got polluted?" Edward said. "Shoot, do a mile before you know it or play pitch the can, see through the water clear like in your bathtub. Now, you couldn't see you hand in front of your face, was you was to put your face in that mess."

"Well, there is mess all over and in politics, it come up to your knees," said Walter.

He remembered his first day in office. He felt so proud. By the time he got to actually be the mayor, in between the election and the inauguration, he had a lot of ideas.

He couldn't help but have them. People dropped by his

house, asking him what he was going to do about so many things.

"I think they should be a commission or department or how ever they call that on sink fixing," said the old lady from across the street who came with her grandson and a fruitcake. "I swear, Walter, I be cleaning my pipes, this boy here can tell you. He does it for me. He's a good boy. But still the drain go down so slow. I think it is 'cause of something in the street."

Walter suggested that she follow the line from her kitchen to her yard before he took this suggestion to his office. "You getting uppity, Walter?" she asked. "Now I'm gonna look for you to announce this in the paper. My baby here will read it every day to check for me."

That was one of the easiest requests Walter got. There was already a department in pipes, except in a different name. But many painful, impossible tasks came, too, that Walter tried to do something about. "My baby," a young mother stopped by Walter's front-yard fence to talk, "he is retarded, Walter. I didn't get the right formula to him when he was a child. Or either it's 'cause of my husband's family. I don't know. But Walter, I don't know what to do either. Since my man left, I got to work and there ain't nobody I can put him with. You know, I don't take welfare, Walter. I don't want charity. Can you help me to get a permission for a school at my house so I can mind him and other children too?"

Her house had been in the wrong neighborhood for zoning and changing it would have cost the city too much money and for her to fight it cost legal fees. Plus she didn't have a degree. Walter still saw her now walking around the streets with her son following on her arm. He thought she was taking hand washing.

"The truth was, what could I do to really help anybody?" Walter asked. "Soon as I come in, the others who were politicians set up against me because I was not one of them. Everything I tried to do, they stopped in the city council. It was like they didn't want me to do anything but parade. Greet the visitors. Pass out the key to the city. Sheet, now if that ain't a lie I don't know what is. Please tell me, what does the key to the city unlock?"

"The bathrooms at the Lake Pontchartrain shelters," Edward said.

"Some room in city hall?" asked Lapin.

"Opportunity," said Jack.

"None of that," Walter replied. "The key to the city is something that if it was smaller you would wear, like a white rose or a red rose on Mother's Day or a boy scout pin. Except those things are more true than what the key means. It means favorites, like you finally got in.

"No problem with favorites, except if you got some that you like, you got some that you don't. Except the city is supposed to be for all of the people and most of the people without the key, the ones you don't give nothing to, you don't even know.

"So look here, Jack, this is what I did to the cause of being fair. I said to myself about serving the people, 'I know what is a true answer, what don't take no councilmens, and I know it won't cost the city a thing.' So any time anyone want to talk with me in my office, when they sit down I play them a song. Then I send them away to think about it, to make up their own mind. And then to do that for everybody, I went back out on the streets."

"What? Walter, that doesn't make sense," said Jack.

"Cents is just only cheap money," said Edward.

"That's right," agreed Lapin.

It was pitch-dark all over New Orleans. Some might say darkness fell all around deep. Out in the country, places like Garyville, Hammond, and Laplace, the evening smelled sweet like invisible night-blooming jasmine and tall grass. The pasture's blades attracted little bits of water from the air. They bedded down with each other clinging to each other in spite of not appearing the same. One was tall, green, and rooted in the earth. The other tiny, round, and a traveler. But it disappeared in the morning as dew.

In New Orleans, the city, the nature of earth was harder to see. The nature of man came first. It was a house-building, singing and dancing being. And, because it was not as easy to understand as the physical world, the man had to search for his truth.

So under the cover of darkness, a darkness of sky solid as a good gumbo pot, conversation bubbled through the night to get at the reasons for everything being. And as anybody would say, that was good.

In the bar, laughter was good too and truly not easy to perceive. "Funniness," as Edward would say, "that's what they call them men dress up like girls." He might add too that, "Yeah, my little cousin was with them, went all the way to France. Came back speaking the language and with a college degree. Made us proud."

Jack had almost given up thoughts of leaving on the plane in the morning. He had also, pretty much, given up fear. Every once in a while he would take in a pause in the conversation. The other men never stopped for even a breath. Jack would have to think about why he was here. He didn't know how to explain to his girlfriend or his parents, or especially the guys, the situation he was now in. It was as if he had know these people all of his life, and they cared for him. But he felt that in any other place or time, they would be opposed.

Jack couldn't imagine sitting in a bar in the middle of the night in Connecticut or, God no, in New York with three big black men who hardly spoke the same language as he did. What would they all have to say to each other?

But here he was. He never spent this much time talking to even his father. "I mean," he tried to think of explaining it, "I spoke to them all day."

Maybe if he told them it was one of those situations like on the *Twilight Zone*, where the hero is captured by his own curiosity and totally forgets his fear. But Jack regretted and apologized to himself for that thought. He wasn't heartless, maybe sometimes confused. But there was no threatening here.

Quite the opposite in fact. But so strange, these men conjured up awful images of each other in words. Jack couldn't picture his father calling anyone a fool without being ready to fire them or walk away from them. Here these men were calling each other terrible things and, seemingly, liking each other more for it.

This was something he'd have to think about for a long time. Or not think about, just let the idea come. These men advocated faith and trust, but not believing. Every once in a while, as they spoke, Jack felt he really understood that there was a genius to that.

"Drink up, boy. You a young man," Walter was patting him on the forearm and encouraging him. "You not going to slow down now, are you? Don't be no chump. I'm about to get to the best part."

"Who you calling a chump, sissy?" Lapin defended Jack as he raised his heavy head to look up.

"I'm calling you, your mama, and his cousin," Walter pointed at Edward.

Edward toasted Walter and Lapin, "That's right."

Jack said, "I'd like to propose a toast to friendship and special times."

"Well, all right, boy," said Walter as Lapin and Edward also lifted their glasses. He added, "As it was in the beginning, is now and ever shall be."

"Amen," Edward said from his habit.

"I'll really tell you about friendship," Walter said. "Lapin let me play here when he opened the first time and I met my wife here . . ."

"His present wife," said Edward.

". . . and there was no better occasion, a trinity of friendship —my woman, my music, and Lapin. The place started to fill up around five in the evening. People coming in after dinner. Most of them work in the trades, you know, so they do everything early from the time they get up. There was even some of my friends from grammar school here, Canard, PeeWee, plus one of my schoolteachers, old lady Judice.

"You know, when I was a child, I thought she was the most beautiful woman. It was the way she treated us, that made her appear like that. By the time I got in high school, I recognized what she really looked like—a straw hat frayed at the brim where she always put the hat pin, stockings twisted around her skinny legs like somebody just spun them, and that nylon dress with the shoulder pads falling down to the front above her flat chest. But that time, when I was a teenager and saw her on the street, I said, 'Good afternoon, Miss Judice.' And she said, 'My smart boy Walter. How are you doing in school?' You know, the sound of her voice changed her in my eyes, like she had been wrapped all of a sudden in a beautiful blue sheet, the color of the lake when we was boys, and thin like a new bride's negligee."

"Damn, man, that's beautiful," Lapin said, resting his face in the palm of his hand, his elbows on the bar. "I had Miss Judice in second grade too. She sounded just like that."

"I think ya'll got some kind of mother thing," Edward joked to lighten their load.

Walter smiled, "You should know, mule."

"Now, don't talk about my best friend or my wife for that matter," Edward said.

"Oh, look, isn't that her walking across the street with that young man?" Lapin pointed.

Edward spun, "I don't see nothing."

"You must have missed her. The guy looked like Creole Clark Gable," Lapin said.

"Sidney Poitier," said Walter.

"Muhammed Ali," added Jack.

"Ya'll joking me," Edward said. "OK, I'm the fool."

"The fool of the heart is a wise man," said Walter. "Let me tell you about my wife. Like I said, when I met her, she came with her cousins to listen to me play. We knew each other as children, yeah. Went to the same school, just different grades. But we never talked. She was always helping the nuns, wiping the blackboard, taking out the trash. And me and them, well, we just couldn't get along.

"I pretty much thought the same about her at that time. You know, when all the little fellows getting their first girls, ten or twelve years old, you don't want nobody you can't feel. So you get you a girl, just as curious, ya'll show each other things, go about your business. This woman, she up with the nuns all the time, I tell the boys, 'She ain't got no appeal.'

"Come to find out, after we married, one of my friends told me he was her secret all the time. I got no hard feelings on anybody 'cause of that, no. So, she had hers. I had mine."

"Tell the man your wife's name, brother," Lapin encouraged Walter.

"Wanda Yvonne Notburga, don't that have a ring? It kind of whispers up on you. Then rumbas. She is really a saint. But she knows what to do with her women things. I don't like to talk about my personal business, but in the bed, she can really make a man satisfied. Not that she don't make you work for it. But she be working too, you know. It's like, very much together, something you doing. I think that's a form of love," Walter said.

"Back to the bar, the bar, man," said Edward. "I don't know how far I can go on this tumbling hayride."

"Hey . . . I might see your wife again," said Lapin.

"Ok, just go on with it," Edward heard him but addressed Walter.

"Anything you want to say is all right, Walter," Jack said.

"Thank you, boy. Thank you also for your attention, peanut gallery," Walter looked at Edward.

"When Lapin first opened and my wife come in with her cousins and I pick up my horn, heaven on earth. Pure beauty. Feeling like falling asleep after you and your good woman have done it, except without no humanly tiredness, only with your blood running smooth and steady like a good tap faucet. That's what it was like to be playing up on that bandstand.

"That's why too, when I was the mayor I took back to the streets with my music. Couldn't nobody argue with anything that is true. Well, some of them could, and did. But I'm getting to that later. First, I got to tell you about my full term."

"Good as dancing the slow drag, wasn't it, Walter?" said Lapin.

"And just as dangerous," he replied.

Jack had never danced the slow drag but Edward told him it was like the two-step except without moving your feet and bringing your partner so close "ya'll forget who stops where."

"As I was saying before," Walter continued, "I took to communicating by trumpet. Like when I wanted my secretary to bring me a pitcher of water from the fountain, I'd play 'Little Brown Jug' or if I was leaving City Hall for the day and I wanted to let the people know, I'd do 'Old Man River' and end it with that part 'He just keep rolling along.'"

Jack put his beer down on the table, "This part you are joshing me, right? I mean I believe you were the mayor. But you played music instead of talking for everything?"

"Well, not for everything. I mean, it was just not fit for everything. When things were important and sad, like that retarded school I was telling you about, and had to be done, I tried to reason with folks. But they wasn't good on being reasonable either.

Seeing how I become the mayor, they stayed upset about that.

"So seem like anything I be for, they be against, and also the opposite. I couldn't claim to do anything big the whole time I was there," said Walter.

"How long was that?" Jack asked.

"In days, hours, or minutes?" asked Walter.

"However."

"About four months."

Lapin spoke up quickly, "But them was the best 120 days ever had in New Orleans by anybody. Don't you see? When Walter was in office there was no taxes passed. The police stayed home. Nobody was starving. Everything was handled out on the streets."

"See, the politicians was against me. But none of the people was. I took my horn to City Hall Plaza outside every day to play. I used to make up these blues, you know. And all the cleaning ladies and the men who stand at the doors in the big hotels would come down and it just tickle them. One I had, 'I may be low. But don't you tread on me. I may be low. But don't you tread on me. I'm the bestest mayor as could be. You wish I leave. But then I think I won't. You wish I leave but then I think I won't. I got in here by the people's vote.'

"Well them people loved it. Whoo, they would laugh. But them on the city council and all the rest of the politicians, I think they was ready to hatch chickens right on that lawn. I heard one of them saying once, 'Frank, we got to do something about that mayor. This music playing is making us laughingstocks.' Me, I stepped up to them. I ain't afraid of no coat jacket wearing fracas. I say, 'If you is laughingstocks, you belong in a stockyard.' And then I walk away."

"That's telling them, Walter," said Edward.

"You got good courage, my friend," Lapin agreed.

"Plus, 'cause they was wrong. I was doing fine for the people. For a good while at least. I tell my secretary, 'We don't need all these desks and these telephones and all this carpet and chairs.' You think I got all that carpet and chairs in my house, Jack?" Walter turned to the young man.

Jack shrugged.

"Well, I don't. Tell him, Lapin. And tell him if any man lives better than I do," Walter looked to his friend.

"It's the God truth," Lapin said.

"So my wife, who runs a good house as any man can tell you, but especially me, she say, 'Walter, I know you been complaining about how all that furniture be collecting dust up in city hall.'

"'Yes, my dearest,' I tell her. She say, 'Well, why don't we give it to the nuns. They help the poor and the sick. And I bet you they could do something with it. So it don't all be wasting like that.'

"Now this here is a woman who could take a penny and buy something with each side. So I know this is an exceptional idea. What be better than to help the poor? And who be more good than nuns? Can't nobody complain with that. Or so I thinked."

Walter refreshed himself with a gulp of beer at this point; right after his glass was refilled quickly by Lapin.

"It's a crying shame," said Lapin, "when people don't follow the good, no matter what kind of clothing it wears."

"That's right," said Edward. "People always want to see the wolfs in sheep's clothes. But what if the wolf in wolf clothes? Most of the time, seem like that to me anyhow."

Jack was a little puzzled by this turn of the story. But he was learning to wait by now to find out what was going on. He sipped his beer more, although he was trying a little to keep awake by this time.

It was about midnight, Jack guessed. He wondered whether the hotel would look for him if he didn't arrive tonight. He was glad he had taken the key offered to him by the desk clerk.

"I bet you that you want to keep this in your pocket," he'd said. "We leave at quarter to three. But lots of times people what got hotel rooms don't ever be using them to sleep, no way."

At the time, Jack thought he was being solicited. He still, at this moment, wasn't sure.

"So man, you should have seen this," Walter said. "Me and my boys. Lapin was with us. Also Edward here. And Bootsie, that's before he was dead, and the St. Augustine High School band and football team and we even had some of them Harry Christians. They said they would pitch in for the cause of the poor people and it didn't make them no never mind whether the poor was helped by the city or them or the nuns.

"I had told my secretary the night before: 'You put all of this furniture what I got a piece of tape on, you put it in the hall.' And I went around all the rooms in the City Hall building. Taping all those chairs that people never sit in and them plushy couches and some of them big telephones and empty water coolers. Anything that look like it never been used or ain't being used enough, I put the red tape on. That was on a Friday. Then Saturday morning, we got in our trucks with all those people I told you about and the football team and the band, and we loaded it up.

"It was a beautiful sight, if you ever wondered about it. Beauty, that is. You tell him, Edward, you is more good with this," Walter said.

"I tell you like this, Jack," Edward began. "Since you been in New Orleans, you ever go to Jackson Square?"

"Yes. We passed by there earlier, today. I guess it was today, right Walter?"

Walter nodded to Edward, yes.

Edward continued, "Well, you know how the bums, they be sleeping in the shade, the children be playing, and mules be drinking water and pigeons flying around. Well, either two things could happen. The pigeons could peck the mules, and the mules break aloose and kick the children, and the children run frightening-like right over the bums. But no. The mules and the pigeons, they drink from the same water, and the pigeons they fly over the children and become part of their game, and the children don't disturb the bums, till they ready to wake up. So they all work together, kinda natural. Well, that's just like how it was on that day.

"Them St. Aug boys be carrying that furniture over they shoulders like book bags and the Harry Christians be putting it up on the trucks. Lapin brought the cold beer for everybody who was of the right drinking age or pretty close. And me, I supervise and Walter play his horn," Edward said.

Walter remembered that day as his best in office. It was the culmination of his aspirations and his wife's thoughts.

"A big crowd gathered listening to the music and started to help when they found out what it was that we was doing," continued Edward. "And most of them, lot of folks, got in their cars and followed us out to the nuns' house. That was Saturday.

"Well, by Sunday, wasn't a stick of furniture that wasn't sold or swapped or something. We got commitments like, a year's worth of restaurant meals for a family of six for one of them twelve-button telephones. Shoot, lots of people wanted the keys to the city. Got a man said he would pick up three old folks a week from the home take them to the social security office for a key. And people paid money. The nuns counted two, three thousand dollars just off of rugs. Do you know how much poor people that could feed, Jack?" Edward asked.

Jack said no.

Walter calculated it for him. "The nuns ain't what you call extravagant when it come to meals. So you figure on beans, rice, and chicken wings. That's about sixty-five cents a plate.

"My sweet wife," Walter said, "was so happy, I thought she'd arise right into heaven when they said they could feed all those poor folks."

Lapin said, "You was the bestest mayor, Walter. The most good-hearted, righteous one of the bunch."

"But as we be trying to tell you, Jack, the truth has its limits. More, I figure from my experience, than lies," Walter said.

"When you become a official politician," Walter explained to Jack, as Lapin wiped off the bar where the men sat, "you can't believe nothing except what you have to at the time. Any other thinking about truth's just wasted baggage. You know, they tie you up. Keep you beholding to something or somebody. And politicians got to be able to change their minds.

"It's like the law. The law says things is one way, and if you don't go with it, you against. No matter that you trying to do good. Good don't necessarily got no part to it. Good is for individual peoples to think about. That ain't got much to do with what the law sees as right or wrong. It's like this fella in jail told me . . ."

"You went to jail?" Jack exclaimed.

"Just for a little bit. Not to worry. Not for too long," Walter said, "Anyhow, this guy in there told me, 'Sure I stealed out of Schwegmann's. I ain't had no job. My baby child was sick. We needed something to eat and we ain't had no money. I ain't did nothing like beat on or hurt nobody. You think that's a crime?'

"'Sure do,' I told him, 'is against the law. That's why they put you in jail. See, I was hungry at one time or another and I never took nothing that didn't belong to me. I played for my money at the houses and such. But that's . . .'

"'So why,' he say, 'are you in here, you so smart?'

"'Well,' I tells him, 'I just thought being I was the mayor, what was in City Hall was mine.'

"See I explained it to that guy like this . . ." Walter went on.

But Jack was looking outside through the window and around the bar. No one was there except the three men and himself. And Jack imagined or realized, he drank so much he wasn't sure, that it was beginning to dawn.

He could hear no sound but talking and maybe distantly a little music was playing. A shadowy aqua-green light seemed to bathe the street. When cars passed they either did or didn't have on headlights.

The room where he sat was wooden and old, as if it had been saturated with years of cigars and talk. You could have put a match to it, Jack figured, and nothing would burn. The floorboards and beams in the ceiling looked plump and swollen. The place reeked of liquor. But to Jack it smelled simply sweet.

He looked at the men he was with. Edward was sort of pigeon-faced, pinched around the nose and eyes and sagging around the rims. Lapin had a forehead that stretched too far back from his eyebrows. It seemed that his whole appearance took a shape swept off from his teeth. And Walter didn't seem at all frightening now, even though he had just told Jack about jail. Walter was not the tough guy that Jack conceived him at the first bar before they all started to talk. Then Jack had him in his mind for a criminal of a certain type.

It was almost as if, in the sodden atmosphere of New Orleans, all the hard opinions that Jack had formed while he was growing up had suddenly become waterlogged and soft. Their edges became blurry, like looking into a fish tank or, even more, like looking out. Jack wished that he had some way to hold onto the conversation, like he had tape-recorded it or something. He wondered after all of this drinking how much would stick. He decided he would catch the plane after all and he could almost hear the sound of his jet landing at Kennedy airport, a high-pitched whistling, sliding down the scale and then hitting the ground. Junk shake. Junk shake shake.

"What kind of music you like, Jack?" Walter was asking him. "I want to play you a song."

"Well, Mozart, the Grateful Dead, Neil Young, Leon Russell, Stevie Wonder . . ."

"Good," Walter said, "I'll make up as I go along." Walter stood in the center of the floor. Empty chairs supported him on all sides. The trumpet began like an old lady humming aloud to herself "Summertime." "'One of these mornings,'" Edward sang softly, even though Jack could still hear him, "'I'm going to rise up singing. Gonna spread my wings and take to the sky. But till that morning . . .'" Here Walter departed into a light staccato tune, sort of sweet. "Hubert Laws," Lapin told him, "Ain't that fine?" Then the beat changed again, one more time accompanied by Edward, beating on the bottom of his chair. It was Brazilian sounding, almost like a rumba. "Go on man, parade," Lapin called. He was strutting from one end of the bar to the other, waving his dishrag above his head. Three steps up, three steps back, two steps, two steps, one to the side. "Go on," Edward called to Lapin, "shake, shake, shake it, now."

Walter held his trumpet down by his side and finished this part singing, "My kind of town. All around. Down in New Orleans, but . . ." he paused. And he began slowly, "'Them that's got will get. Them that's not will lose . . .'" He picked up the trumpet again and played with the words Lapin stopped and sang, "'so the Bible says, and it still is news. Your mama may have. Your papa may have. But God bless the child that's got his own.'" And the song changed again, and Lapin moved with it as if he had been doing this for many lives. "'I've been so many places in my life and times. Sung a lot of songs, made some bad rhymes. Acted out my life in stages. Ten thousand people watching. But we're alone now and I'm singing this song to you.

"'I love you in a place where there's no space or time. I love you for my life, you're a friend of mine. And when my life is over, remember when we were together. But we're alone now and I'm singing this song, singing this song to you, to you.'"

Jack applauded. And so did Walter, Edward, and Lapin.

Plus, Lapin snapped the air with his dishrag and Edward wiped his eyes.

"What was it like in jail, Walter?" Jack asked.

"Black man, very, very, very black."

Walter moved back to the table. "I don't mean in color, not at all, even though it was us mostly who was in there for one reason or another and that makes you think too. But man, what there was was an absence of sound. The door close behind you with a clunk, you know, like slamming the tailgate of a truck. Except it be you in the truck and there is no open top or sides.

"Sure there is talking, plenty talking. But most of it is quiet and all of it is words. Even when you would hear guys screaming or fighting, it come at you like if you was breaking a glass. It was those kind of sounds, nothing good that I heard."

"Come on, man, let's not talk too much about that. It's all over and done," Lapin said.

"Well, you know, kinda," Walter replied. He took Lapin's dishrag and wiped off his horn.

Edward said, "Tell him about when you went to court. Now boy, that was a scene."

"Like Mardi Gras," Walter said. "I was just trying to do good, selling that furniture. The people, they knew, that was just me."

He continued, "Them councilmens, they was the first ones. And I sort of think my secretary was in on it too. When I come into my office on that Monday afternoon, they was all standing in there waiting, saying, 'What the hell's going on here.' One of them tells me, 'This is public property.' And I say, 'Well, that's what I thought, so that's where it goed.' And another one of them said, 'You done broke the law, Walter; we knowed you was going to tear your drawers some time.' And I tells him, 'Well, at least I wear some. Who know what happen to yours.'"

"I'll tell him this part," Edward cut in. "So they got sheriff and such and law and bring him to court. But sheet, child, we pack up that room with more people than they got seats. And all of them seats in there, all was permanent. You know, nailed to the floor."

Lapin picked it up, "They was lined up against the wall, thick as thieves on one of them Arabian Nights. Had the newspapers, the televisions, the grandmas, and the babies in there. Had the high school boys and the nuns. Remember," he called to Walter, "Sweet Percy came with all of his girls."

Walter said, "Sure do. Looked like a flock of parakeets in the front row in they yellow evening gowns, red business suits, big blue matador coats. And they hardly let the judge get in one good word.

"'I'm going to have to put all of ya'll in contempt,' the judge said," Walter reminisced.

"'Contempt my behind, baby,' one of them called out. 'Tell him girl. Speak the truth, darling,' said one of Sweet Percy's boys.

"Well, man, that whole court was just a laughing. Some of them old ladies brought picnic food. All of the time the council-mens was up on the stand, the old ladies be wrapping and un-wrapping they brown bags and wax paper. 'Shush,' the officers kept trying to tell them. But you could hear those old girls whis-pering back asking them, 'Honey, you can have some if you want. Don't you? This is good.'

"Well, of course, I got to get up in front of the people. But I ain't ashamed. I did what was right and I got some pride. When I'm walking up to take the stand, somebody in the back blow one of those big plastic horns, you know, like they got at football games. 'Baraam,' it goes. The police hustled that fool out there quick. But everybody had to laugh on that one.

"I say, 'Yes sir judge mister. I realize now it was public prop-erty. But the nuns, they just can't give it back.' The sisters, even old Mother Ignatius in the wheelchair, is sobbing, pulling they handkerchiefs out of their sleeves. I say to the judge, 'Look at them. You ever seen a more pitiful sight?'

"'Walter,' he tell me, 'that's not no question. You done broke the law. The sisters neither the Harry Christmas is public, you know that. So now you just got to go to jail.'

"'But am I still the mayor, your honor?' I ask him.

"'I'm sorry to tell you, Walter. But you ain't even got that.'

"Then my lawyers go talk to them other lawyers and whisper up with the judge in his robe chambers. And when they come out, he say, 'Hear this, ye everybody. This here what we going to do. Walter, to keep us from all being the national laughingstocks, you just go to jail for a few days, pay back the money so we can buy some new furniture, and we call that that.'

"'But your honor,' I tell him, 'I'm unemployed. Where I'm going to get the cash?'" Walter leaned over to the young visitor. "Jack, if you don't remember anything ever, remember, what comes around goes around," said Walter.

"He don't need no lecture," said Edward. "Tell us the rest."

"Well, don't you know, when the judge bang down his hammer, all the people begins to boo. Hollering, 'That ain't right.' 'This no kinda justice.' Mother Mary Ignatius, she even throw up her fist.

"But next thing you know, as me and Wanda leaving the courtroom, people start handing us dollar bills. Some never said nothing. Others whistled, 'Come over here.' I must have got two, three hundred dollars from each one of Sweet Percy's girls. Of course, Sweet Percy hisself, he don't give me a dime. In fact, he come tell me, 'You just a fool. Need to be in jail.' My wife, she look at him in the eye, tell him, 'Jail is in the person. You already inside your own walls.' I separated them. But I swear, I was sure proud of her every minute since that. That's a good woman, Jack. She tell what need to be told, when it need to be. You try to remember it."

Edward began talking. "Damn if they ain't had the pilgrims over to his house for months after. You know lines, just like the holy shrines running from his yard down the street."

Walter said, "Yeah, people dropping by bringing me quarters, fifty centses, fat ladies bringing me plate dinners to eat. Shoot, we had more than enough money to give back to the city then. They fix up City Hall like the lap of luxury. But after we returned the cash, and we were broke again, you know, we still felt rich.'

"My wife say to me, 'Walter, we got love and memories plenty.'

"'And music,' I tell her, 'You can't never forget that.'"

The sun surely had risen by now, Jack thought. He could see bright rays painting the floor. Whether that light would bleach the wood or make it look stained, he didn't know. But then, he remembered, it moved evenly all day, from one wall to the other.

Edward had gone to the bathroom. "Oh Lordy," he said.

"Getting too drunk with ya'll. Made me forget all about my mule." Lapin was just about finished washing glasses. He planned to leave in a half-hour, he told them, "Soon as I get my relief."

"You about ready to go, young son?" Walter asked Jack, "I'll walk you over to your hotel."

Jack said, "I'll wait for you outside. I'm going to get some air." He thanked all the men and he promised to look them up when he returned to New Orleans. He was definitely coming back.

Jack stepped out of the bar and looked to one corner, then the other. The street was practically empty. It must have been about 7:00 A.M. He could hear trucks passing with a "Vaaroom" on nearby blocks. He thought, probably delivering sweet corn to the French market he had visited. He saw in the slight morning fog the vague shadows of old ladies turning every few minutes or so into the doors of the cathedral. He wondered for a little while if it was important for him to know why they entered. A couple of men holding hands walked past across the street and waved lightly at him. He returned their greeting with a slight nod and a smile. A tall woman in a bare red dress approached him from behind, strolling, it seemed, with her mother. The old woman told him, "You ought to do like I tell her. You young people don't listen. You got to rest yourself once in a while."

Jack took a deep breath and walked with a drunken sway to the corner, his hands in his pockets. There was so much to think about. He looked at the pavement, then the street. The cement was cracking in places, showing old brick. In the middle of the block, across the road, he could see one of the eighteenth century markers plastered onto the building. He went over to read the sign.

It began, "In this house in the 1780s lived an African of French descent . . ."

Edward and his mule passed at the intersection. "All right. Take care, boy," Edward called.

". . . who from all accounts was a tribal leader in his home town . . ."

Lapin sped by in his Volkswagen.

". . . and in New Orleans became a popular figure uniting

white immigrants—Irish, Spanish, French and others—and blacks. His profession was not known. But he is believed to have been at different times a musician, providing entertainment in Congo Square, or an educator or storyteller. Legends also recall him either as a sorcerer or a saint. His name is the cause of much dispute among historians because it was translated into so many local languages. But he was called mostly . . ."

Jack saw Walter walking quickly in the other direction of the street on which he was standing. So he ran stumbling to catch up with him. But the man turned the corner and when Jack finally reached him, it was not Walter. So Jack tried to return to the bar.

But he had turned so many streets, he was a little lost. He couldn't figure out for the life of himself where he was. He wandered around searching for the bar until people began filling the streets, going to breakfast, church, shopping. Finally, Jack got in a cab.

"The hotel, please." He looked at his key to make out the address.

"Where you from, boy, with an accent like that?" the driver asked him.

"New . . . Connecticut. I'm from Connecticut."

"Well, isn't that nice, you visiting us. Oh, here come on the radio a good record. I'm going to turn it up a little. You don't mind, no? Music. I swear, I live for music. I'm telling you the truth. What about you? You do that?"

CLIMBING MONKEY HILL

IT WAS CAUSE FOR EMBARRASSMENT IF BLACK children climbed on Monkey Hill, even after they had integration. The boys and girls who ran from their nearby homes to play in Audubon Park after school did not arrive with their freedom only given by the law.

When they ran up the hill, they were ridiculed by the parents who called down their own pale children. The adults stared at the black ones as if to see them for the first time. Although some were their over-the-fence neighbors, they replaced with bitterness the casual greetings of earlier times. "Look at them little monkeys on Monkey Hill," the parents agreed to each other over their children's heads. They spoke in a jovial way that encouraged their sons and daughters to adulthood by sharing the laugh.

Watching from a distance away, Levia knew what occurred. The adults stood confidentially close to one another, but arrogantly. Phrases of sarcasm carried to her in the air, although only slightly because there was no breeze, as is usual in New Orleans in summer. Levia did not expect to hear more of their words, because to shout at the children made the adults appear reckless under the law. She recognized they used their only remaining tool, ridicule, and, legally, the children were not bound to care.

Still, she held the hands of her brother and sister to keep them away from Monkey Hill. "Don't let yourself be a joke for nobody," she told them, just like her mother.

Levia's mother warned them not to wander too freely while she walked to get soft drinks. They were all safer if the children stayed on the blanket she placed on one patch of grass while she alone went to the concession stand.

But Levia now told her brother and sister, "Here, take some

money and go get on a ride," to make them feel better. She wanted them to know they could afford to go places. And she watched their figures walking away, like miniature adults hand in hand, little shadows of a man and a woman walking across a horizon sharp as tightrope while around them the world offered itself bleached and bare in the midday sun.

Levia sat on the scrap of lawn looking at Monkey Hill. It was a big lump in the middle of a flat, dusty field of Audubon Park, like one bucket of sand a child upends at the beach. Any grass planted once on Monkey Hill had died from the heat or underfoot from children running. Before development in this area, the park was a corner of swamp near the Mississippi River. It still had in spots the aura of unforgettable melancholy like most of New Orleans. But it took on an irony. Huge oaks with moss waterfalls fringed the dry field where Levia sat.

Monkey Hill was an even more incongruous site on the barefaced and dusty plain. Mud and river sand piled up about three dump trucks high, Levia figured. She pictured men in white uniforms building Monkey Hill and molding it with their hands like a giant, clay ice cream scoop. After Monkey Hill took on popularity, politicians on television proclaimed it a site for the education and freedom of enjoyment of the children of New Orleans. Levia knew who they meant.

Anyone offered something by television in 1965 had to be only one race. And that specification excluded Levia, who was many things, but not white.

She was a girl who now at adolescence molded her two fat plaits into one rope of hair that followed her long neck and turned up naturally where her shoulders took hold. She was nearly as tall as her squat mother and glowed healthily like her dad.

"You're a miser's penny," he told Levia to let her know how precious and beautiful she was to him. She was copper-colored sometimes when he looked at her. Other times she showed more red or gold. He teased her, "Maroon," like that kind of person sold for a time in New Orleans after she ran very fast. So Levia was actually black and as yet a threat to the people who wanted only one kind of child on Monkey Hill and in Audubon Park.

But that didn't bother Levia. These days she cared less about what people thought and more about what she was feeling. Specifically, she wondered if Monkey Hill was high enough to see New Orleans in a different way.

No one in the city, adult or child, who did not travel ever experienced both going up and coming down another side of a hill. The closest they ever got was the levee, which extended itself to one high point, then made a sheer drop. A child running against the breeze had to stop suddenly at the peak of enjoyment or fall into the river.

Levia once went alone to the levee. At the plateau was a path where people rode barebacked horses or walked south to the left and north to the right. Levia wondered how far they could go before the levee was no longer needed, either because the earth held back the water enough by itself or the waves of the gulf took over.

Levia wished she could go to the river now. The day was so hot and uninspiring. The adults that Levia and her family joined in the park now bickered at a picnic table a hundred yards away. The topic, as usual, was who got hurt in civil rights demonstrations this week, and how everyone else should react. Levia just wanted to go some place where it was high, quiet, and she felt free. At thirteen, she wasn't anxious to join them.

Her mother said Levia should begin making decisions. The first one she gave her today was to watch the children near Monkey Hill. "Olevia, mind them till I come back. Show a little responsibility," her mother said. Levia felt responsible already. But she could not talk back. "Yes ma'am." That's all she was allowed to say as yet.

"Yes ma'am. No ma'am." Who gave Levia credit for thinking? She felt she considered a lot but everyone said she was daydreaming. "Just a stage, you know," her mother told people all the time to explain Levia.

Levia had stared out the window this morning while they drove to Audubon Park. It was about one half-hour from their house.

The scene changed from small wooden homes that were painted to match the same shades in their gardens to half-block estates with stained glass windows and ironwork.

While they loaded the car to leave—shoving in the blanket and ice cooler along with a box of sandwiches their mother promised to bring for her friends, the neighbors came out to their porches and watched. They nodded approval, or showed envy at the picnic by waving down to them like shoo-fly as the car drove off. The children were bound out of respect to reply to either greeting.

"Hello, Mrs. Dee. Hi, Brown. Good-bye, Irma Ann." They had to catch each personally or the one they missed would try to convince even the others who got a hello that the children— because they were going to white places now—were growing stuck up.

By the time they neared Audubon Park, they could quietly look out the window. The houses here were so big, even if people wanted to they couldn't wave to their neighbors because no one could see another from porch to porch.

Everyone called this area the garden district because the big plots displayed huge flowering trees. Not only did hundreds of flowers grow there but almost as many people were hired to take care of them. Levia's father, who knew people that worked outdoor parties in this area, said anyone black who wore a uniform was welcome here. In this neighborhood, no one flinched at the mention of slave quarters attached to a house.

Levia studied those estates in the city magazine that her mother ordered to come weekly to their home. And when she and her mother drove around, exploring the city, as they did often, Levia counted streets and streets of these massive and imposing buildings. Some had four big, square, brick front-porch pillars, that her mother called, "grandiose Creole." Others had smooth, round, white columns, "southern Greek." Shingled roofs came down low to just top the cut-glass front doors that sparkled like diamonds. Levia liked to believe these doors were locked like the treasure trunks in her mythology books and held great mysteries and came from secret places. But Levia's mother reminded her as they drove that everything she saw was the product of "hard work." And, occasionally, as they passed the houses, she said, "Slave labor."

But she didn't say that often because it stopped both of them from talking and she knew Levia liked to dream aloud.

"I'm going to have a big house on St. Charles Avenue someday."

Her mother said, "You better learn first to keep clean."

"And I'll have a library of books in two rooms and a horse in a stall near the back by the park."

"And who's going to pay you to waste time?"

The conversation usually developed into an argument soon after that or else Levia's mother ended it quietly, "My child, you can have anything that you really want."

Except recently, Levia wanted to go to the garden district by bus and walk around by herself like she did in her neighborhood. But her mother said, "That won't do." Because of integration, people in the city were angrier with each other than ever before, especially when they were separate.

Levia considered going without telling. Their anger had nothing to do with her. She'd have to change buses and streetcars three times. Even the transportation system allowed for the separate traditions of New Orleans communities. Different people did not live side by side. Instead, their houses were back to back. So there were white streets and black streets and most traffic followed the major white avenues, where Levia thought to get off and walk.

If she went on the bus, on entering she got a thin piece of tan paper to make the transfers. She had to be careful not to clasp it too tightly or sweat because it could melt in her hand. Many seats would contain workingmen who smelled strong from their day jobs and women with their arms draped tiredly over the back part of the chairs where their small children sat. Levia had to avoid the old ladies because no matter who sat next to them, they talked and she could miss her stop.

For the first transfer, she would be on Canal Street, where she could see anyone. A neighbor might tell her family. A stranger might hurt her. There were sailors and tourists, shopgirls and businessmen, teenagers much worldlier than Levia and foreigners who wanted to stop and talk. But people said that was pointless because they were dumb. Levia wasn't sure whether that was actually true. But it was safer, she felt, not to speak to anyone at all.

At Canal and St. Charles, where she boarded the streetcar,

there would be a crush to get on. But by Magazine Street, all the pushy ones—men from the business district, transients, and the women who shopped in the expensive stores in the daytime, but who lived other places—would have left. Those remaining stayed in either big St. Charles houses or the small communities organized to serve them, located a couple of streets behind. But both of these people accepted their destinations with leisure. Some pulled down the wooden shade and dozed out of the sun, as the train rocked on the tracks to the end of the line.

The problems, Levia imagined, would only come when the streetcar had only a few empty seats. A great deal of confusion occurred about who would sit first since the curtain was gone behind which black people sat. Now if a seat became open, a white person might come to the back of the bus to claim it or a black to the front. Both movements were considered rude if others in the predominant race in that section stood. Even a young boy would not get up for an old woman, unless they were the same.

Once Levia's friends rushed to a seat to prevent a white woman from sitting. "Come. Here. Olevia," they called. "You shouldn't stand."

Levia kept her head down for the remainder of that ride while the others joked. She felt she couldn't look up to see the old woman, swinging on the strap and panting for air in the hot bus. Levia repeated to herself, "Slave owner. Miss Anne. She's not so fragile." Levia wondered then, would her mother think this was rude or just?

Levia did not want to encounter trouble if she went by herself but she did want to take the ride. She knew her mother would say, "No. Everyone is just too upset now over integration."

Integration, that's all Levia heard and she was sick of it. New Orleans became possessed with the idea. It seemed good enough to think about, when it was planned. But now it just appeared too much trouble to Levia.

People were always protesting and others moved from places they lived all their lives. Where blacks and whites had lived willingly with their differences, now they were bitter. Too much change, Levia thought. Too much fighting, supposedly because of their children.

For years, Levia looked forward to high school. But now the

first question everyone asked her was whether she wanted to go to school among blacks or whites.

Next summer she'd have to make up her mind. "Does it matter?" she asked people who looked dumbfounded when they heard her reply. That was another occasion when her mother asked everyone to excuse her child. Then whoever posed the question to Levia in the first place would say she had a duty to her race. Of course, she had a duty. Levia understood that.

For what other reason would she be going to school at all? Lynne Carre's parents let her wear miniskirts and boots and date boys who were five years older, and Lynne said she wasn't going to school because she first had to please herself. Actually, she was pregnant last fall.

But Levia's parents "expected things" of her and a baby was not part of their plan. If fact, her father warned, "If I ever see you on the corner with those neighborhood bums, don't come home." So she didn't stay out late. Not that she thought he was fair. But she believed he would not let her back in the house and she couldn't figure out how she would take care of herself alone.

But everyone else made too big a deal of things she would do naturally, like go to high school, while Levia had better plans. For example, Levia made herself a promise to enjoy living day to day. And she was keeping it, not worrying too much, thinking about the things she wanted to do and not the requests of others, remaining free like a child.

She thought, this was the prime of her life, the summer beginning, and she was in the park. Levia lay in the sun, idly thinking, alone without her sister, brother, or mother. She took the quiet for granted, rested and watched the shadow of Monkey Hill grow as the sun marked time.

"New Orleans has too much of a mixed-up society to be bothered anyway," Levia heard one of the adults talk against integration at the kitchen table one night. "Now, who's going to tell me how they going to draw the line around here?" The grown-up said no one would want real race relations legalized: "With where the poor whites live and the St. Lima whites with black people from Corpus Christi Parish right back of them, politicians going to be zigzagging that color line all through people's front porches to keep everyone separate and still follow the integration law."

Levia listened to only this part of the conversation, then she went out into the backyard. Maybe it was unnatural to force people to change. She wouldn't mind people keeping a friendly distance like she did with the white country people around the block. They were a family of six pale, big-boned boys and girls whom she really didn't mind.

Once their pet armadillo climbed under her fence.

"Watch him, watch him now," the oldest boy told his sisters as he ran around the corner to get into Levia's yard. The armadillo buried itself into the mud where the chain link ended near the ground. The girls poked it with a stick to send it to their side. But their backyard was concrete. And the armadillo acted as if it were embarrassed to run away but obligated to go where it was greener because it burrowed under the grass behind Levia's house while they called it, going deeper and deeper into a hole.

The boy arrived with a wood and screen box, the kind, Levia knew, that was used to keep pigeons in. He stopped the armadillo by cornering it with a board. He kept blocking its moves until the animal tired of the places it originally wanted to go. Then he picked up the armadillo and showed it to Levia, "Look here." She studied its slate-colored shell, long fingernail claws, and little unprotected parts around its legs on the underside.

"Won't hurt yer," he said by way of thanks. "You could come play with it if you want." Levia shook her head yes to be polite. But it seemed too unfair to both man and animal, she felt, to play with something that you had to catch.

Instead, in the evenings she played with the children in the houses that faced hers on the block. They attended the black public school up the street or went to Corpus Christi, the elementary attached to the church.

Their games were mostly inventions, like Coon Can where they hit a rolling ball with a stick and ran back and forth from one square drawn on the ground to another, scoring points. They played Red Light to see who could sneak to the light before getting caught or Fassé with everyone keeping the ball against one another and a Hide-and-Seek called I Spy.

Before night fell, all the children sat on the steps and talked.

Levia felt they made their own sidewalk family, besides being in-volved in separate ones at home. Elanore wanted to be every-one's mother with her bossiness, "Girl, you ought to take off that short skirt with them bony legs," "Johnson, come over here."

Philip was "doo-fuss," the children said. He allowed his mother to tell the barber to cut his hair too short and one time he even showed them a part shaved crookedly right onto his scalp. Philip never spoke first to anyone and only talked back to Elanore if she pushed up against him. Once he told Levia that when he grew up he wanted to be a policeman.

"Why you want to do that, to have a gun?" she asked.

"I'm sick of white people telling us what to do," he replied.

Levia looked at him hard for a few minutes, then took up con-versation with another child on the step. She didn't tell anyone Philip's desire and she even avoided Elanore some after that. Le-via wasn't quite sure why. But Elanore, Levia sensed, would force Levia to choose sides. And all Levia knew was that she felt bad talking about white people all the time, as everyone did, and now she didn't feel good either talking with Philip.

Levia preferred to spend time with her cousins. Charlene was a cheerleader now for St. Augustine. The two black Catholic high schools, St. Augustine and Xavier Prep, had a football ri-valry so intense that nothing else mattered for weeks in the neighborhood.

"Go, St. Aug," people called from their porches to youngsters dressed in purple and gold. Young mothers balanced their baby children on their hips as they stood outside the St. Augustine schoolyard fence watching the band practice in cavalier helmets. Girls not yet pregnant lingered with one arm hooked above their heads in the chain link to display themselves to the male musi-cians. Many a trumpet and saxophone player was inspired to further a musical career by the sight of female S-curves on the horizon, a line that stretched from the school's Hope Street to Law Street boundaries.

The night before the game, Charlene gave Levia and her friends a demonstration of cheerleading in the street. The boys who wanted to watch promised to keep an eye out for oncoming cars. Levia and the girls sat in a pyramid on the steps and waved their hands like paper shakers for Charlene to begin.

"We're really rocking them, really rolling, really pushing them down the field. Look at Purple Knights, a real swinging deal. We push them back, and roll them back, and knock them to the ground. Look at our team, we really rocking them down. St. Augustine. Go St. Aug. St. Augustine. . . ." Every time Charlene said St. Augustine, the girls on the steps put their hands on their hips and directed their shoulders from one side to the other, like mini-Supremes.

Every cheer these days was a little angry with a newfound pride. Black cheerleaders had always done the latest dances and "finger-popped" while the bands played. However, they got a greater appreciation for the way they looked while dancing after they saw new, sophisticated female groups on television. But they also got laughed at during cheerleading competitions against the white schools. Where their cheers were acrobatic, the blacks' cheers were musical. The result was that the cheerleaders for St. Aug, Prep, and many others held their heads with a little higher tilt under bouffant hairdos that took advantage of their full hair, and they smiled a little less these days for every occasion.

On the day of the game, Levia accompanied Charlene. Then Levia took a seat near the top of the stadium. The air was clear and cool, hinting of the arrival of fall. The oppressive heat in summer that made a poor choice of any seat close to the sun was gone.

Levia looked across the field to Xavier Prep. Bodies rocked in unison as if pulled side to side by the music. Levia heard from the competition an occasional shrill snatch of trumpet or a couple of drumbeats. It gave her a sense that she wanted to dance too. Except she felt it inside, like a stirring in her body or a shiver in a place she could not locate. While she waited for the St. Augustine band to begin, she pulled against the collar of her sweater in a way her mother disapproved because she said it would stretch. But that made Levia relax a little and she looked more closely at the stands below her.

People brought umbrellas to open and bob with the band's music. Others waved handkerchiefs in their enthusiasm. Like two hundred flags, an army of individuals bound by music and rivalry, they slapped the air to the right and left.

The movement was one of sureness. Levia felt part of a single voice raised for enjoyment of the day. Support for a team was so unlike Levia's picture of high school, if she had to go there under the laws of integration.

When she watched television at dinnertime with her parents, the white people protested blacks coming to their schools. "Two-four-six-eight, we don't want to integrate." Levia saw their spokesman address a reporter, "They will lower the standards in our classrooms to where our children couldn't learn anything."

"Why do we want to be where they don't want us, anyway," Levia asked her mother.

"For the future, Olevia. Pass your plate." She went on serving dinner.

Levia's father said, "Education is the only way to move up. Whatever high school you go to, Levia, we want you to apply for college."

Levia remembered complaining, "Do I always have to think about this?"

But alone at the football game, Levia conceived an easy picture of high school. She would go to a black school and be safe, just like she was today, or all her life in her neighborhood, and with her family.

From her seat, away from the crowd, Levia saw her neighbors—Philip and his mother, Elanore and her boyfriend. Many other people looked familiar to her, like cousins, in shapes with rounded shoulders, in sun-lacquered hues and clothes she knew from the local stores. She nodded hello to a soft, masculine face that she recognized from the neighborhood or was even related to. But when he smiled, Levia saw from the crookedness of the teeth and the way the lips were hooked around them, he was no one she knew.

But he rose from his seat a couple of sections away and began walking over to her. Levia didn't know what to do. If she moved away, he would think she was rude. Plus, she already was sitting at the top, so she would encounter him if she tried any route to leave. She waited, pulling her sweater across herself with both hands, making an X. She was shivering when he arrived.

"Are you cold? What's your name?"

"I came to the football game with my cousin," Levia replied.

"I'm Roger. Want me to get you warm?"

"I have to go to the bathroom." Levia got up.

"What high school do you go to?" He caught her arm.

Levia shook herself away, rushing now, down the steps. She called back, "I'm just in eighth grade."

Levia hurried with her head down and her arms across her chest, to the bathroom under the bleachers. It was dimly lit and where ceiling lights were broken in places, electricity buzzed in the dark. She slowed her pace to think in the dark places because no one could see her there.

She wondered if she could hide from Roger and if she returned to her seat if he would still be there. She was angry because he touched her arm. She wondered what she would do. He can't make me talk to him, Levia thought. But she knew she felt bad because of her confusion. Other girls, like Elanore, could have been slick or jive.

"Does that feel good to you," Elanore had once replied to a boy who had pushed her up against the house. She told Levia, the boy let her go right after that. "I didn't have to fight. You just got to be smart," she advised.

It was just like with white people, Levia thought. Always someone was telling her, "We have to outsmart them to get what we want." When people told her that, Levia could not remember a thing that she wanted from whites. How could she want anything that people were not willing to give? And if she got it because she was smarter, why didn't she have it all along?

Her mother said civil rights was a problem for white people, because "then they will have to see we're the same."

A cheer went up from the stands above Levia's head. This year Xavier was winning. The championship moved between it and St. Aug because they were so evenly matched.

Levia stood still and looked around her. Pretty high school girls flirted with boys in the bright places near the concession stands as they waited to get treated to soft drinks and sandwiches. They laughed with their faces tilted up, just so the light flattered the curves of their cheeks and slid over the bones in their jaws.

Levia considered that men challenged women just to see who would win. Another cheer broke from the stadium above her head. Levia tried to laugh like the girls did who were standing under the light. But she only succeeded in making a dumb sound like little grunts linked by a strained desire.

Suddenly people came running down the ramps of the stadium. "They say there's a bomb in the stands," someone yelled as he passed. Levia looked around for Charlene or anyone she thought she might know. She saw no one. So she ran with the crowd, out of the gates of the stadium into the parking lot.

People stood around looking confused and disappointed. Levia walked from group to group, peering into them to see who she knew. When she got farthest away from the stadium, she saw a motorcade coming. With horns blowing and convertibles alternately speeding up and screeching to a stop, crowds of white teenagers drove past shouting to the people who were leaving the game, "Dumb niggers. We fooled ya'll dumb niggers."

More protests were on the evening news during dinner. This time, mothers were crying and fathers were mad. "How can my child be safe anymore in her classes?" one woman said, full of tears.

"They just don't want our young men fooling with their girls," Levia's father called at the TV from his seat at the kitchen table.

"Marvin," Levia's mother told him, "please hold your tongue in front of this child."

"I'm going outside anyway," Levia told them. "I don't see how no boy can do anything to a white girl that he wouldn't do to me."

Ever since the game Levia was wondering about the rules of being kissed. Was it like something you said you wanted to do? Or was it like being ambushed? People in the movies clung to each other, the man holding the woman's head in his hands as if something precious was there. Levia would have to think harder, like the women on TV, to be able to say the right things and get kissed for her smarts. She resented that people thought white girls would get kissed more than her. Levia felt she had just as much brains.

The question of school, too, still hung before her. But worst, her parents wanted her to consider going to a white school with all girls.

Levia saw them many times on the bus. They wore white blouses where the ironing seemed to melt by the afternoon and blue pleated skirts that they rolled so short it called attention to their legs, yellow like chicken parts. Their mothers let them shave to their knees and many carried big, square, adult pocketbooks.

The girls at Xavier Prep were not nearly as free. A hint of wiped-off lipstick carried three afternoons of cleaning the nuns' windows, and any objection to punishment made necessary a trip to confession.

"You're not going to school to socialize," Levia's mother told her, "and you might make a few friends." That time Levia walked into her bedroom without answering. She did not tell her parents either about the boys she saw pass in the car. She knew they would say "rowdies come in every color."

She was losing her arguments, too, about all white people, because the whites who stayed in the Catholic schools had to agree with integration. The bishop threw out of the church that year any of the others who did not want to mix. It was un-Christian and un-Catholic, the bishop said. Levia and her mother had seen it on television, and they cheered as the bishop refused to talk to the people who protested blacks entering.

"Finally, somebody is putting their foot down on real sin," Levia's mother said. "It is never too late," Levia agreed. But now, as the decision acutely affected her, she wondered, what about blacks who did not want to go to school with whites? Was it as bad for black people to be against white people, as whites were against them?

Elanore said no, once when Levia asked her. "They be always on our case. Why you so polite to them? You some kind of Oreo, black on the outside, white on the inside. Or oleo, yellow all the way through."

Levia answered, "I don't like white people."

"So let's go then," Elanore called her along.

Levia had said, "I don't like white people," a little louder than she would have liked for her parents to hear. They told her because she had freckles from one Irish great-grandfather, that she should not be quick to draw lines. "You just focus on what is just and what is unjust," her father told her, "and don't choose your sides by the color of skin."

But wasn't it true that white people hated them because of appearance? "So why," Levia argued, "do we have to be nice?"

"It will keep you from being a fool to the wrong kind of people, girl," her father said like he didn't want to hear anything more.

But that day with Elanore, Levia did not hesitate to follow Elanore's convictions. She was dark and she had freckles too, like they could be sisters, she said, as she once flattered Levia.

"I know how we can get them," Elanore whispered after they entered Richards, the dime store around the corner on the white street. "I'm going to make a fuss with that woman at the cash register. You pick out some candy for me."

Levia got a few Tootsie Rolls, some gum, and a mint. Then she walked to the front. "That's the one with her," the saleswoman called to a man coming toward Levia as she saw Elanore run out of the door. "Check her pockets. You got money to pay for that?"

"But it's not for me."

"You think I'm going to put it back on the shelf?" the saleswoman glared.

Levia left with her pockets empty of change and a bag of candy in her hand. As she turned the corner, Elanore appeared from behind one of the shady oak trees. "You got some gum for me? You are some sucker." She stood with her hand on her hip laughing at Levia.

Levia drew back her arm and popped Elanore in the face with the candy bag. The candy flew out of the bag as it broke and stayed spread over the sidewalk because Elanore chased her all the way home.

When she got to her house, Levia went straight to her room, to be alone and to be quiet. Both the whites and her black friend had turned against her and she did not want to be around anyone anymore.

"Some people just want to stay stupid," Levia's father, with a drink in his hand, badgered her because she refused to discuss anymore where she was going to high school.

"Maybe I'll just get books and read at home," Levia said.

"Oh, what we got here is a separatist," he called to the air. "You into black power or white?"

"Daddy, shoot." Levia left the room.

She didn't think she could learn at home. But she saw many people on television who took their children out of the public schools. Black parents who feared violence and insults took their children to schools formed by church parishes. Whites who didn't want theirs to mix formed small teaching groups at home.

All these adults claimed to be right. Others said, "Trust in God," for all answers. "His justice will reign," said one woman who came to Levia's door selling religious books. She dropped to her knees and prayed on Levia's wooden porch when Levia told her she'd better start to go home because the radio just predicted a hurricane on its way.

"God's going to whip the slate clean," Levia's neighbor, old Mr. Gontier, stopped to tell her on the way to the grocery store. He had seen many hurricanes, "Lola, Darleen, Sylve, Ethel, Darleen." Levia nodded her head with each one, especially for the hurricane he mentioned twice, thinking he might get the message that she had to go and was getting bored. But that just seemed to encourage him to go on.

"Out of respect," her mother said pay attention to old people. So Levia felt caught by his stories, and she blamed her parents for her delay now. "God always work in mysterious ways. But I'll tell you, He always send a message for you while He's doing it. Something for you to learn from." Levia was beginning to back away from old Mr. Gontier, and he noticed. "Now you hear me well," he hollered. She had backed off far enough to be able to turn her face away, with one last shake of her head, "yes sir."

Levia hurried to the Circle Food Store. The lines were long. Before any hurricane, people stocked up on canned food and candles, liquor, water, and ice. If she ran out of money, Levia wondered which of the necessities she should choose out of that group.

But her mother gave her enough to buy two bags of ice and four tall votive candles. They had enough, Levia guessed, of the rest.

While Levia waited in line, she watched old people gather under the arches right outside of the entrance door. Circle Food Store was more a tradition in the neighborhood than a full-service grocery. It was a rambling building, erected in parts, like occasional Spanish memories, probably as the owners got more money in their cash registers. With several red-tiled roofs and upside-down U's linked side by side to make an open wall for a breezeway that extended over the sidewalk, the Circle gathered the old and the romantic. Nothing in the vicinity was new. The check out clerks were over sixty-five, the pigeons that lived under the arches were balding, and some boxes of food were usually damaged by rain or outdated and sold at discount. The floor was worn in spots from black-and-white linoleum squares to a smooth, sloping plywood.

That the old people came to the Circle in numbers to discuss the hurricane seemed right on time. Levia thought that a good wind could destroy either the building or the people with one gust. The idea made her wish that she had spent longer listening to Mr. Gontier.

"We will be closing in twenty minutes," an announcer said. The checkout clerks sighed and people began rolling their baskets quickly in Z patterns up the aisles. The way their carts jingled over the floor as the people shoved them, then crashed into others when their drivers left them, struck Levia as funny. "Miss, will you hurry up. Is something humorous here?" Before Levia answered, the clerk said, "Next."

The sky was dark by the time Levia reached her house. There were marbled patterns above her of black and white, changing constantly with an unpredictable pace. "Thank God," Levia's mother stood on the porch. They closed the door and latched the long, cypress shutters behind them, just before the wind began shaking the wood.

First it rained like a thunderstorm, except without lightning. Then the wind hit the front of the house like someone was throwing debris. Soon a noise rose like all kinds of people shouting at once. But above it, Levia's family could hear parts of the house next door bursting against its own windows, garbage cans rolling down the pavement, car horns going off and on like bleating—sounds that made Levia think of the instruments in a band running away from the musicians. Tree branches scraped down the street like fabric being ripped. The lights went out.

Levia, her mother, brother, father, and sister moved into the same room and gathered around one votive candle. "First, let's say a prayer for the people who will suffer through this," Levia's mother said. "For the good and the bad, may they find Your Wisdom." The family said, "Amen."

The next morning a neighbor from across the street rattled the door blinds to wake them. Levia's father jumped from the floor. "Man, I thought you were the hurricane," he said after he opened the door.

"You got to see this, brother," the neighbor pointed to the corner as they walked away. Levia ran down the steps to follow.

Water tapered off to become level with the street where it rushed into the drainage sewers about two blocks from Levia's house. Beyond that, St. Bernard Avenue was a canal. People launched skiffs into it and paddled downtown.

"They say it gets deeper and deeper farther back. To the ninth ward, it's over the roofs," the neighbor called to her father over the sound of others saying the same thing.

The street was also filled with children playing. They laughed and splashed in the shallow water as if all of a sudden God gave them a public pool. The city had ordered all swimming facilities closed a year earlier since too many people complained about such intimate mixing of whites and blacks. Levia's mother spoke to the television when she heard the reports, "That's OK, city, we always swim in the natural lake."

Neighbors slowly returned who had left their houses to stay with relatives during the storm. They carried stories up the street, crossing from porches on one side to those on the other. The telephones didn't work. So they had the only news for everyone.

"In the ninth ward, the water is over your house," one man said. "They claim lots of us drown." He carried the contents of his refrigerator, offering meat and eggs to families as he went along "I rather do this," he said, "than to let it spoil."

Levia went to the corner to find other children. Only Philip was out. "They say Elanore's family went down to the ninth ward."

Elanore's grandfather approached her house dressed in the suit and straw hat he wore every day to go to the horse races.

"They not home," Philip said and told the grandfather about the floods in the ninth ward.

Elanore's grandfather sat on the step with his head in his hands, "It's the white people."

Levia went to the edge of the water at St. Bernard Avenue and waded. Then the water got too deep, near the curbs where the street sloped down or near intersections. So she swam. The water was brown like the river and it smelled like the London Avenue sewerage canal. People passed in small motorboats, making soft wakes. They shouted, "You ought to get out. This water's filthy."

But Levia wanted to swim downtown as far as she could. She could go two miles in the lake and had since she was little. This water was shallower and porches jutted above it along the way where she could rest.

Once when she stopped, bits of clothing and then a suitcase floated past. "Didn't get away fast enough," Levia thought, then she wondered where was the person they fit. The water held boards and tree branches, plastic toys and food, like a box of cereal. Levia watched most of the day from that porch about one mile from her house. She did not go further because all she saw ahead of her was just drifting and she decided not to just follow along.

When the radio came on in a couple days, reports said the levee had broken downtown. By that time, Levia and her family already heard a different story from people arriving in boats docked near their street. People said the levee was torn away by the city at a section in the ninth ward. That made the water pour into the black neighborhood and relieve the flooding of whites on the other side. Everyone who drowned during Hurricane Betsy was black, Levia heard. A movement began for revenge.

Elanore never appeared and Levia prayed constantly, asking God to forgive her for hitting Elanore in the mouth. Soon after, she saw Elanore getting out of a car. Levia ran up to hug her. "Is you crazy?" Elanore jumped back waving her hand at Levia as if to drive away a bad smell. "Nobody got to worry about me, I could swim."

Elanore's mother told Levia that Elanore saved her grandmother as the flood rose. She pulled her in the water from the roof of a house to the three-story school building across the street.

"I'll tell you one thing, I'm not going to be nice anymore," Elanore said.

People sat on their porches more than usual for the next week while the telephones were out. Daily came news, less about dead people now, more that pet cats were bloated and found in backyards when the water receded, or new furniture was ruined with no insurance to pay for it, and of permanent watermarks near the ceilings of houses.

Where Levia disbelieved everything before the hurricane, now she listened to anything. "They say the Black Panthers are going to defend the ninth ward from now on," Levia told her mother, "and they're going to stop school integration."

"Cheer up," Levia's mother smiled. But Levia could not figure out what she meant. Levia was frightened like most of the old ladies she visited on the block. One told her, "I guess God just don't want people to mix. If He did, wouldn't he see to it that we could get better along?" Levia thought for a second that her father said people were together more at one time in New Orleans, until they started black and white separate justice. But Levia said nothing. The old woman kept talking, "I think them Black Panthers is right. We need protection."

"The Panthers say, if you don't put something black on house, you have no respect for the dead in the ninth ward and you will be hurt," Levia brought a new rumor home.

"That's crazy," Levia's father answered. "Who doesn't know we're for black people doesn't know us. So it's none of their damn business."

But in the same way as Levia brought that requirement to her house, other children and childish minds spread the rumor down the block. The neighborhood soon accumulated drapes of sympathy all day in varying degrees from solidarity to fear. Flags of red, black, and green hung out of some windows. In others appeared pieces of black material, a coat jacket, a navy blue towel, and a negligee.

"What is she giving up for the revolution?" Levia's father called to his wife.

"Hush up," her mother laughed.

Levia followed her father into the bedroom and watched while he opened a dresser drawer and got out his gun. "I can take care of this family good enough."

But when they went to sleep, Levia took her grammar school uniform out of the closet. Although it was navy blue, she planned to hang it out on the porch. She unlatched the shutters and pushed the blinds open to see if anyone was outside. But the electricity had not yet been restored so there were no streetlights.

Levia tiptoed out to the porch, clutching her school uniform in her folded arms over her nightgown. To think of a place to hang it she sat on the steps. She tried to get her eyes to adjust to the darkness all around her. She could make out a few lit front rooms in the neighborhood where people sat up, or where they left the lights on because they were afraid. Levia felt cold sitting on the steps in her sheer gown. But she didn't want to go inside.

There was something going on all around her, and Levia felt if she sat outside long enough she could smell it. The air held the salty moisture of breeze off the river, the rancid smell of moss and wet grass, and a tinge of something burning. Levia thought to hang her school uniform on the door. But then she remembered that she would have to wear it tomorrow and her father would be the first one out of the house. She thought maybe he was right about keeping the gun loaded. If the white people came inside, he would just blow them up.

"The big fish eat the little fish, and we, the people, eat all the fish," old Mr. Gontier joked with Levia as she watched him unload his boat. His nephews stood in the skiff on its bed pulled behind the car parked in the driveway. Mr. Gontier handed one of the older boys the garden hose to wash the stench of dead bait and catch out of the boat, while the other gave him the ice chest.

He dragged it into his unfenced front yard and took out fish one by one to show the children. "This here is my dinner. And this," he picked up a dead shrimp, "was his dinner." The children laughed as he made gulping noises and pointed to the fish.

But some fish were still alive. The children stared at their big, unblinking eyes and sighed while the fish drew air deeply through their gills. These produced a collective "Aw," in sympathy, speckled trout that lost their rainbow as soon as they were lifted out of the ice by the tail and croakers who made long, painful belches as they gasped to flop slowly from one side to the other on the pavement.

"Ya'll too soft," Mr. Gontier fussed at them. "Where ya'll get hamburgers? From Old McDonald's cow!"

"Ugh," children groaned and covered their mouths. The old man continued, "And you know how they kill them, pow, they shoot them right in the middle of the head."

"I don't believe you," Elanore said. "Old stupid man," she called ahead of herself so he could not hear from behind her back as she went home. Levia decided it was time for her to go too. Philip remained next to the step until the sun went down and the old man said he had to go inside.

Levia went to the kitchen table, "Do we have to kill animals to eat?"

Her mother replied, "Well, there are some things that we grow. A person could eat vegetables and grains all the time."

Her father entered the room, "No. Listen to me child, in life, you are either the hunter or the hunted."

"That's not true, Marvin," said her mother.

"You tell me why then, if it's not man against animal, it's man against man. It's either kill or be killed, Darwinism, the philosophy of the hunter. Have people ever been able to get away from that? No, it's a jungle and until people first understand that it is, they will never get beyond it."

"Well, that's the survival of the stupid if you ask me," Levia's mother said.

"Thanks," answered her father. "What are we having for dinner?"

"Pork chops."

Levia ran out the back door, holding her stomach. "The poor pig."

Twilight was falling when she sat on the backyard steps. She tried to make out the outline of the things she enjoyed. The bay-leaf and pecan trees, the tomato bushes, her mother's planters with pansies, the doghouse and the dog's silent pacing in his fenced off section.

She heard evening bugs around her. Something big like a bee flew near her head and she tilted her ears on an angle to the ground, and held herself stiff. After she relaxed, she stared at the dark grass. Its stillness was calming and every once in a while, she'd notice a faint little glow, a lightning bug, low to the ground. Levia stayed outside even though the mosquitoes were beginning to bite.

In the daytime, mosquito hawks ate the mosquitoes. Like fly-ing dragons, someone once told Levia, mosquito hawks were all over the yard. She used to catch them by their transparent wings and feed them tobacco. Now she just liked to watch them. They were getting too fast for her, Levia's mother said, to encourage her to act more like a lady. And Levia began to take pleasure just noticing their prettiness. The mosquito hawks had different tints; some were shaded blue, some green, others black, silver, gold from their flat, fly noses to their crispy wings.

If she caught them, she did not see the color. She had to con-centrate on keeping them still. Half the time the wings broke from the pressure of children holding. Most pinched the wings harder if the mosquito hawks tried to get away.

Once Levia's mother caught Philip shaking a mosquito hawk by the fragile wings to make it release the tobacco in its mouth.

"Philip, what are you doing? You gave it to him."

"Ma'am, I don't know."

"That thing didn't do anything to hurt you. So leave it alone."

Levia wondered as she began to go inside and slapped the mosquitoes now stabbing her arms if it was all right then to kill something that first comes after you?

She hit at the site of a prickly pain and squashed the insect

into a fragment of rolling fabric under her hand. When she tried
to pick the dead bug off her arm, what she felt most was the wet-
ness of her own blood.

Her cousin carried a gun with him all the time. "Once I was
fishing," he said, "and I nearly got bit by a snake." He was a big
man and a hunter like most of his friends. Sprouting along the
walls of their houses were necks, faces, and antlers.

He taught Levia how to shoot. "You don't have to act all the
time like a girl," he said. "Besides, you'd better learn how to
protect yourself." He placed his hand over hers as she held the
base of the weapon. "Now hold it straight up and shoot it into
the air."

Levia pulled the trigger. A vibration traveled from her wrist
to the center of her chest. "There you go. Now that wasn't bad,
was it? You want to do it again?" he asked.

Levia said no. He had shown her the proper way to load and
carry the weapon. Shooting it once was all she could stand.

When he let her shoot, it was New Year's Eve night so no one
noticed the ringing sound. In fact, shooting rifles and handguns
was part of the fun in New Orleans. In neighborhoods where rifle-
men did not have time to buy blanks the sky rained buckshot.

Everyone drank and hugged out of tradition in the background. Overhead was pitch-black. But the shooters stood safe
distances from each other, or in groups that would not face head-
on, and from the ends of their weapons, quick, deadly fires
blazed. It was like one hundred matches lighted at once, or a
burst of anger, a scar on the sky. Levia wondered if the woods at
night stayed black and lonely only to protect itself.

The children that year played a new game called "Killer."
One girl's cousin brought it from California for the holidays. He
lived in Watts. They would sit in a circle and wink at each other
before another winked at them. Once you caught the wink of another, you were dead.

Levia played once and lasted a long time. But she did not like
the way she felt during the game. "Come on, girl," the boy from
Watts challenged her, "I could do better this time and it's more
fun with lots of people."

"Didn't I tell you I don't want to play?" Levia pushed his

shoulder away from her in the circle where they sat. But before he could push her back, tears came out of her eyes. She did not know why and they dried up immediately from her own shock.

The boy walked away from the other children, telling the others, "Where did you get this weird one?"

While the party was still going on, all the children were called into the front room. The television was on. "Look at Dr. King," the grown-ups were pointing. It was more news about civil rights, Levia thought. She didn't want to listen too long. But everyone was quiet. He was talking about marching for non-violence. He kept using the words "Love" and "Peace."

"He don't know these crackers down here in New Orleans," one of the adults said. "I rather listen to Malcom X." Then the adults began arguing and Levia returned to the other room. The children were talking about the same thing. "I'd rather see them all die," the boy from Watts said, "than to live with them."

By spring of her eighth grade year Levia had to start thinking about high school. Elanore would attend the junior high in the neighborhood for a couple years, she said. Philip told everyone his father wanted him to work.

Levia stopped going around them because they kept asking her what she was going to do, and bragging about their own choices, which Levia felt they had not really made. If they were telling the truth, she told herself, how were they able to decide so easily?

Surprisingly, in one year, some parts of the the city had gotten more accustomed to integration. But now pressure came from other sides. Her teachers encouraged Levia to be the first. "Go there and get on the volleyball team." Or, "It would be nice if they had a black girl debate."

Levia would have to fight for these things as well and she was not sure she even wanted to try. Others in her community showed her another way: That blacks did not need to be among whites at all. That made sense to Levia from the life she had experienced so far.

A man visited every Saturday morning selling *Muhammad Speaks*. He talked to Levia's mother at length each time. She liked the way he looked. He was dressed out-of-date as far as

Levia was concerned, hair cut too short, a bow tie and a suit that was too shiny, especially for Saturday morning. But Levia enjoyed the way he paid attention to her.

"Good morning, beautiful sister," he addressed her. "Is your mother here?"

On days that her mother was busy, he handed Levia the paper to bring inside and her mother swapped back to him the weekly newspaper of her Catholic faith. Levia wished she had something intelligent to say to Brother then. She had always sneaked out of mass off and on so they couldn't talk about that. But in *Muhammad Speaks* she had read the cartoons that called "shameless" the women who wore their dresses too short and tight. Levia had not yet developed a figure like in the cartoons but she did feel she could comment on that.

So the next time Brother came, Levia tried to seduce him into a conversation about clothes. She was standing in front of the house watering the garden. She was barefoot because of the especially warm spring day and had on a short playsuit. Every few minutes she would run a stream of water across her legs and feet. That stopped them from scalding on the cement for a time.

"I think you are right about women not wearing their dresses too tight, Brother," Levia smiled and looked him in the eyes.

"That's right." He watched from the blush on her shoulders down her long arms that ended at her thighs to her toes. "Are you cool or warm?"

"OK, I guess. But I think it's right about self-respect and the way ladies put on dresses. My parents always told me that."

"Is your mother home?"

"No. But you can talk to me."

"Give her this, beautiful sister. And if you want to have a conversation, there are many women who would like to give you guidance, if you wish to consider visiting the Mosque. In the meantime, young sister, be aware of yourself, like your mother says, and at least put on a dress."

Levia felt very hot. The soles of her feet burned. Suddenly she realized why. She had been standing the whole time with the water running into the bushes. She picked up the hose and now pointed it at the cement as the Brother left. Then she held it up like a fountain and let it shower her like when she was a little girl.

Charlene called to ask Levia what about going to St. Mary's. If she did go to St. Mary's like her cousin Charlene, Levia might be popular. St. Augustine picked most of its cheerleaders from there. It was a black, Catholic girl's school and having a cousin could help, especially since Charlene was awarded the title of school queen during her senior year.

Levia considered the possibility of an active social life based on her royal blood. She remembered Charlene's coronation in the auditorium. Folding chairs covered the floor except for a wide center aisle. Parents sweated in their Sunday clothes. Some women wore tall white hats iced with net in their high school sororities' colors, while men had on shiny striped suits and several kinds of official emblem ties.

That day Levia sat on the aisle so she could photograph Charlene. Everyone smiled as much as the queen did as she passed them to the stage. Charlene was as gracious as if they all were her servants applauding. She waved her scepter like the bishop sprinkling out blessed water with a holy enthusiasm that the people shined under like they were catching some summer rain. Levia wondered if everyone felt like she did that Charlene was looking just at them and if they looked back, they would have some of her beauty.

When Charlene arrived at her aisle, Levia snapped a picture and waved. Charlene stopped then and blew Levia a kiss. A sigh rose from the crowd, sweet like candy air floating up to the sky from the cotton-making machine. It was as if everyone puffing softly could make Charlene nicer.

Charlene got the most roses, red long-stemmed ones, of any of the girls on the stage. The runners-up received flowers according to rank and Levia took pictures of each one of them, even though the man sitting near Levia said, "Save your film for the best."

Later, after the photos developed, Levia pinned them to the bulletin board on her wall. While she studied and listened to the radio in the evening, she stared at them every day until she knew by heart what they all looked like.

She imagined that these girls were like starlets who were kissed in the movies, each one more favored than the next. The ones who were the least pretty were the least admired. The one who was beautiful, Charlene, was not only well-liked, but rich and famous.

But the day Levia was studying and thinking about going to high school and she looked at the pictures, an idea occurred to her. She was not nearly as pretty as Charlene. Levia glanced quick to the mirror; there was hardly a family resemblance. How would they know she and Charlene were related? And what if she told them and they could not see Levia was as pretty as her cousin, so they didn't care? What if people didn't like her still after they knew she had a famous relative? She would be a total failure.

Levia suddenly felt like a little fish in the high school pond that was already eaten by Charlene. What could she do to change this fate?

Levia sat still thinking with her hands on her books and listened to the radio. It played the Supremes' "Nothing But Heartaches." Then the Temptations came on with "Just My Imagination (Running Away with Me)," and then followed a new group called the Jackson Five.

Levia had danced to this music by herself many times around the room, pretending that she would grow up to be somebody that a special person would like. No one like that had yet arrived, although a kind of love life happened already for some of her friends.

Like Elanore. Levia hadn't seen Elanore for months. But someone told Levia that Elanore was sighted on Canal Street. "She was sticking out this big." That person put their hands right about in the spot of a beer belly.

"Who is the daddy?" Levia asked.

"Who you think," the other said, "Philip."

Levia wondered now how someone like Philip could be a good father at all. The men she imagined herself dancing with were at least a foot taller than Philip, broader and had deep voices.

"Why haven't I seen you before?" one whispered to her.

"I guess because I'm inside studying a lot."

"There is nothing I like more than a woman with brains." The handsome man pressed his hands softly against her head and tilted her up to kiss.

"I can spell constitution," Levia whispered back, "C-O-N-S-T-I-T-U-T-I-O-N." She returned to her lesson. There must be some benefit for spelling.

Her eighth grade teacher said that men liked women smart as much as they liked them pretty. Levia as yet saw no evidence of that. She saw that men just wanted the pick of the best women. But then they all had their definitions of best. She had asked Philip once. He said, "I like them sexy." Brother said that women should not be sexy at all. And her father just said, "Stay a good girl." Levia did not know a woman yet whom she could be like and yet not compete with. Everyone wanted to tell her how to grow up. But Levia thought the grown-ups made too many rules about life, just like the white people.

The white people said blacks were lazy and ugly, athletic and stupid. Levia knew that didn't apply to her. So why should anything else?

The radio announcer said it was 5:45. Looking out of her window, Levia felt that was about right, although she could never guess the time in early evening when the sun was no longer visible but the sky wasn't yet dark. It might actually be only a few minutes long. But Levia felt she spent several hours of every day in twilight.

Perhaps that was because she sat so long thinking about everything lately, particularly herself, not nearly as grown up as she wanted to be, but much more than a child. She was tall and lean. Her face had pushed out in places that promised to be attractive. Her body even showed little bumps and curves, plumpness where she was once all hard running muscle.

But her thoughts seemed to grow only in spurts, then completely shrink, so that lately she had no control over her mind. Where she once had contentment, peace like her little brother and sister had who played and hummed all day to themselves, Levia now was uneasy. There was nothing to do. Nothing could hold her interest. Nothing satisfied. All one day she spent worrying over a cowlick that appeared in her hair, until her knees ached. Her mother called that growing pains.

If hurt meant something was growing, Levia thought, so was New Orleans. Now people were breaking the windows of government buildings and setting houses on fire, in response, they said, to the hurricane. New Orleans ached all over from integration. Levia didn't know if it was worth all that much. Why couldn't everything have stayed soft and comfortable like when she was young and a baby?

Then, the family went on picnics out at the lake. In a special place, Levia learned to swim, between two identical pilings. They were actually broken telephone poles hammered into the lake's bottom for a construction that never came. They were the same because the tops of both of them had been split by lightning.

She was just a baby when her parents let her float inside a life preserver tied by string. They sat on the shore, on a step that rose out of the water, letting her paddle out with the soft tide, then reeling her back in. Only once did she get in trouble, when she drifted against a construction piling. She bumped it and tried to hold on. But her parents tried to pull her back, thinking she had just grazed it and was not clinging.

The life preserver got caught on a nail, holding her just at water level. Every time a wave passed her head went under and she had to hold her breath. She screamed for her parents in the wake of the water, when the low, sucking part of the tide came. A couple of times, she hollered too late and a salty flood filled her nose and mouth, and she was choking.

"I will die now," she remembered thinking. "My life is short." But she actually had no choice then. Her mother arrived to take off the life preserver and wrap one arm around Levia to pull her to shore.

They continued swimming that afternoon, Levia's mother said so they would not become afraid. Her father, who never learned to swim, stood anxiously watching from the steps while holding the string and life preserver. From the water, Levia could hear him continue to curse the broken pilings and construction wood junked in the lake's "colored side."

Levia remembered those years when the lake was divided into separate areas where the blacks and whites swam, that the white side had a sand beach; they could see it when they passed in the car. On the colored side, a slope into the water was built with tossed off street construction material—bricks, rocks, and broken oyster shells.

At the time, she thought the shells where pretty. But her cousin, the hunter, said, "That's because you were a kid." Levia wondered, if she went to the colored side of the lake right now, how would she feel about it?

Levia's father got a phone call from a man on his job. "Stay out of trouble," the voice had warned. Her father had told the family at the dinner table. He made a joke out of it, "I was in trouble just by being born. I don't know what side's doing the calling." He explained at his job, there was a continual fight between blacks and whites. "I try to stay out of it until it gets to me," he told the children. "Then I got to act."

Levia saw him in the morning, getting ready for work. He was taking his gun. She volunteered to get it for him. "I know how to handle one," she said.

Levia lifted the case from the drawer of her father's dresser. She set it on the bed and unzipped the leather holder. It opened like the inside of a small animal slit up from the belly to the throat.

The body of the revolver was a metallic brown. Levia brought it to the light to see it up close. With the white bulb shining hard, the gun appeared a mean grey, the color the bank looked that night when she and her father got there too late and were locked out.

She heard once on the radio that everything living has colors, like emotions. Peace is green and anger is red. She wondered how she looked in the light of the bedroom lamp, if it had the power to diagnose her feelings as it did with the turncoat gun. Levia wondered if people turned colors when they were afraid. Would a crowd of people marching, if incited, suddenly turn orange like a clamoring flame?

And were the colors of rage and happiness the same for white people and black, or were they darker and more melancholy for black people since they seemed sad more of the time? Or were colors just reserved for the halos of saints, glows that surrounded their heads on top of their hair?

As she was thinking, Levia loaded the gun for her father, to do him a favor. She took out the box of bullets from a different drawer. She broke the revolver like her cousin showed her and spun the chamber, putting in bullets one at a time like thumb tacks.

People have to defend themselves, Levia thought. If they didn't, who would? She thought that her mother would answer the question with God. Her father would say himself. Levia wondered who would defend her if either one of them died. Would she get married for her husband to protect her? Nobody like Philip would ever do, she thought. Nor would anybody who didn't think I was pretty enough.

Levia continued to load the gun slowly and carefully. She could hear her parents arguing in the back of the house.

"Are you crazy, you going to be like the rest of these crazy men. Shooting at shadows? What is going on with you?"

Her father said, "I just got to show who is the boss around there. If I don't show some strength now, everybody will be able to push me."

"But a gun, Marvin," her mother said. "Isn't there something else you could do?"

"I thought integration was the answer. Hell, I pushed for it at the job. And now, everyone's turning against me."

Levia tried to listen now. She felt alone too most of the time. And for some reason, she was always afraid. But afraid of what? Certainly not whites. Not blacks. And yet something was always bothering her. Something that made her anxious. It was a feeling like a weak stomach. But she carried it around with her all the time, as if it were already a part of herself. Like no one could give her the definite truth, the right thing to do, yet they were asking her for it. What's good for the future? What's bad for it? Do you want to live around whites? Do you believe in killing for a just cause? What are the limits of race?

It was as if all the adults she knew became suddenly stupid but they continued to act. Big people shouting on television that they didn't want children to go into a restaurant or ride a bus. Her father kept his gun oiled. Her neighbors hung underwear on their porches now every time there was a thunderstorm. The city said it could not figure out how the levee broke.

And all of them were asking their children, what should we do? You are our future now. It seemed to Levia that the children were their present, were responsible for their own life and death decisions. Levia looked up from the gun, saw the picture of Charlene smiling from where she was pinned on the clothes closet, and then Levia couldn't ignore her own reflection in the mirror.

Maybe the truth always weighed on children. Mama said when she was a child she had to raise her brothers and sisters while her parents worked. She had to cook and clean and get them from school every day. She had to defend them from the bullies across the street, she said too. Once she said she hit a boy in the head with a baseball bat. "I never went to see what happened to him," she told Levia, "and I heard he was OK but I regretted it all my life."

"But wasn't it him or you, Mama?"

"The older I got the less I could tell."

Levia had just about gotten the gun loaded and snapped the barrel back into place.

Then she reconsidered. Her father just had to show he was powerful. So he could take his gun. But she would protect him. She would finally make a decision that would help her parents.

She opened the gun with both her hands, pulling the barrel apart from the body on both sides. She shook the bullets out to the floor where they hit soft like hail. Then she went into the back room where her parents argued.

"Here, Daddy," she gave it to him. He put it inside the waist of his pants under his coat jacket. Levia felt good all day. She had made a decision. Like Martin Luther King, Jr., she thought, she would tell her parents later, she had decided on nonviolence.

She felt good until her father did not come home that evening. While she and her mother waited with dinner, they turned on the news. "Oh my God, Levia," her mother called her close to the television. There were pictures of violence and sounds of shots as the camera weaved through the crowd. "That's Daddy's work," her mother said, "What should we do?"

Levia didn't know what to say. She just ran out the house. "The white people," she said to herself, she kept repeating. "They killed my father."

She ran to the corner where the children were playing. But she had nothing to say. They just looked at her as she stood silently. She ran to her cousin's house, the hunter. But he wasn't home. "I'll get a gun and I'll kill them," she kept saying to herself. "I'll kill all of them." She ran around the corner where the white children lived. She shouted to them on their porches, "I hate you."

The boy heard her and came down the steps. "My father," she hollered and she began to run home. He followed her and by the time they arrived, people from her neighborhood were all gathered around her steps. Everyone was saying, "What's wrong?" They were talking to her mother who was looking for Levia. "What's wrong?"

"My child," Levia's mother gathered her close and held her. They sobbed together on the steps of the house, while all the neighbors came near. The people were there from the front street where the blacks lived. And the children from around the corner brought their mother when they heard the news. "Oh my God," they were all saying, "dear God," when Levia said she had taken the bullets.

Then her father drove up.

He thanked everyone for their concern. He had gone to another location for work. There was too much fighting on his job. He had expected the worst and before he got out of his car, he checked and found his gun wasn't loaded.

"Then I asked myself," he told the neighbors, "what if my child felt responsible. What if I killed someone. Everyone now is too crazy. We have never hated each other before like this." Old Mr. Gontier called from the back, "Amen."

"We got to act more civilized," he said. Then he opened the door of the house. "Anyone who wants to is welcomed inside," he told them. Slowly, the neighbors came in.

They entered all night, filtering in and out. People talked from the separate streets who never knew each other except by appearance. They introduced themselves by name. Mostly, the black people stayed. But the mother of the white country people from around the corner came bringing all of her children.

Levia made sandwiches, opened soft drinks, and cut cakes that people brought and served them around. As the crowd stayed in the back room of the house, the children her age gathered off to the side.

While they talked, Levia asked the others where they decided to go to school. Nobody liked where they were going, and they wanted to stay in the neighborhood. The white country boy said most of his friends left the public school because they were afraid of the blacks. Levia said she did not know where she would go yet, "But I think I want to go where it's integrated."

"Why?" someone asked her. "Everyone just wants to fight now. Isn't it just too hard."

"Not everyone," Levia said, "and only because things are important."

When the people were leaving the house, Levia thought she wanted to ask the boy more, about what things were hard for him. She wanted to ask him if he had ever climbed Monkey Hill, and how did that feel. She thought maybe the next time. But not too long after that, his father moved their family out of the neighborhood.

And as time passed, Levia began to think less about the games of Monkey Hill played by children, the running and climbing and fighting to get to the top. And she thought more about growing up, and how in the future people could be good, but not better than others.

BEFORE ECHO

MORNING LIGHT DOES NOT ENTER THE SWAMP.
Even the sunrise is dark. Still, time progresses, night into day.

A picture of bayou country is deceiving. Slow streams converge under mud to make the appearance of land that is actually water. One net of moss hangs from one hundred trees. Lightning strikes the same stump many times.

People pass the swamp's fringes in trains, on tracks that cling to the last solid ground. Out of their windows are landscapes that take the earth's colors to every periphery. Bright orange sunsets surround people like sky on an airplane. On grey foggy mornings, they ride through a dream that has no beginning or end. But time has its limits, these people know. They are expected places—Memphis by midnight, New Orleans by dawn.

Deep in the swamp, animals keep the only appointments. Birds gather at high places in trees. Raccoons make their last noisy passes for food across someone's back porch before he awakes. Fish all around splash up although they cannot see the morning coming to clean the picture of day like clothes bleaching in a galvanized tub from dark grey to light grey.

Joan looked out from the porch to the swamp she had known all of her life. Ahead of her in the veiled light were the outlines of many trees. Below and around her were the crisp sounds of nature awakening. Cupped in both hands, perched on her knees was a warm mug of coffee.

Joan got up early for no other reason than habit. If she stayed in the bed, her bones would have felt strange. To avoid their odd aches and stiffness, she rose when the dampness of morning settled on her face. She could smell the dawn since the air held a less stagnant pungency.

Usually the smell of rotten wood and dead fish came into her house. It mixed with the smell of moss, moldy but flat. But it provided a diverting aroma when Joan put her face close to the pillow or mattress.

The house was surrounded on three sides by water. Joan looked for her reflection when she first arrived on the porch. It stood out on stilts like a dock. But she did not see her appearance. The water was too dim and the morning too early.

"Is the same now as it was then, before the Savior, before the words in the Bible," Joan spoke out to the darkness and considered that little had changed since the very beginning.

Joan thought and dreamed a lot lately because she was so much alone. Her life was proscribed by the length of the days, and the bounty or scarcity of food in a season. "That's everybody," Joan reconciled her existence as the same as everyone else in the world. Perhaps she was more lucky than most to be fitted so well with nature. Everything she needed was inside her home or within the boundaries of water.

Her ideas differed little from the rare people who still lived in the swamp. When the fish ran, the oysters grew fat in their salt beds; the animals' furs thickened with the anticipation of cold; the people prospered and prided themselves for remaining in exile like their forefathers had in tribes and from Canada.

Joan didn't know history or think about it because she was still young. Her life was the present. Even the Bible she read, although written hundreds of years earlier, spoke directly to her.

Joan lived with her grandfather and she took his ways too as modern behaviors. She hunted and fished, repaired the house, and sewed crab nets. She sipped homemade wine, smoked pipe tobacco or sometimes chewed it. It occurred to Joan only rarely that other young women might not live as she did. But if she considered that briefly, she dismissed it.

When Joan sat on the porch in the morning, she waited for nothing. Now she wanted to hear the buzz of outboard boat motor that would tell her the doctor was coming. Joan's grandfather was sick.

About illness, Joan was again like the swamp folk who took sickness too personally. They saw failure in themselves or the removal of love by the Creator. That was one reason few people remained so isolated. Not many could sustain such passions with the invisible.

Joan wished for parents in her times of trouble. But they existed for her only like the dark spaces on the other side of the trees. Joan wanted to feel in the big, empty clearing, peace and the comfort of nothing. That was her idea of belonging. When she was a baby, Joan's mother died, her grandfather said. They were not ever acquainted with Joan's father.

The woman at the supply store that Joan reached by pirogue boat suggested that Joan try to find out more about her mother and father. But Joan told her, "I don't care." The woman tried to convince Joan, "But what if you could know them? Don't you want to know?" Joan said, "Non." That was her lie.

Joan had tried early in life to figure out more from her grandfather. But her mother was like any daughter, Joan's grandfather said. That's all he knew. Joan worried, "How I could find out? Who I could ask?" But there was no one around her. And the concern made her days in the swamp go heavy and slow. When she began to feel that some fault caused her to be alone rather than God's act, Joan suffered. It was painful to think something should have been changed. Joan's only solution, she realized very young, was to not think about it. Only then could she experience comfort in her days that consisted of chores to take care of the house, the dog, and her grandfather.

Joan did not venture further with her curiosity, just like at night she did not go beyond the porch. Other animals saw better in darkness. Then, they took over the land and the water. Joan only heard them outside and from their weight, she guessed they ran in packs or danced in couples, that her only recourse was to scatter if she saw them in daylight.

Joan felt the darkness allowed the animals to conceive and to multiply. The darkness inspired God in His time to create the world. In Joan's darkness was quiet and mystery. She kept the time before her and of her beginning in ignorance.

Joan heard the faraway sound of the doctor's boat for ten minutes before he pulled up to the house. He handed her his bag before stepping from his rocking skiff to her stairs going down to the water.

"How you how you?" he greeted her, just like the people he visited, although they bragged he "had education." They took credit for his success because he returned to them after going away to school. They boasted to each other of his ability to move between the worlds of "smart people" and "us."

Joan's grandfather now remained in the bed separated by a fabric curtain from the rest of the house. Joan could hear his breath whistling loud like a person who sleeps with a cold, although he didn't rest. Sometimes he just stared ahead toward the door and his eyes rolled back toward the ceiling. Joan was afraid.

The last time the doctor visited, her grandfather did not awaken as his pulse was taken and the doctor placed the cold shiny thing over her grandfather's heart. The doctor made Joan listen first to the old man, then to herself, and then to him. "You can see for yourself. I'm sorry to tell you the truth, but he ain't doing too well," the doctor said. Joan held the object deep to her grandfather's ribs to hear the faint swishing and patting not quite in rhythm like clothes on the line being blown by the wind against the side of the house.

Her own heart in contrast sounded like her bare foot tapping against the planks of the porch. And the doctor, even though he was much older than Joan, but younger than her grandfather, his heart thumped like the dog's tail on the floor wanting to be let out.

After the doctor left, Joan talked to herself about the Bible and read it aloud to the dog. She unwrapped some dried fish from a piece of paper and took some leaves from where they hung in a bunch near the ceiling to make a thin soup. She tried to get the old man to drink. But most of his food drooled back on him. She drank the rest on his plate and gave some to the dog. She sat on the floor near the old man's bed. And she held his hand as he had not allowed her to do since she was a little girl. She was now sixteen.

Joan noticed her grandfather growing old when his thick hair turned flatter, and from black to grey, white, then yellow. He walked slower. But since they traveled few distances by foot, she didn't care.

A few years earlier, she had raced to their summer bathing

place by the inland river and he could not keep up. But she challenged him less often as she got older. So they walked there in a slower, actually elderly gait.

She was young and she was pretty, Joan could see in the water's reflection once the light had descended in a flat heat and the darkness erased. But she did not especially flatter herself. Joan washed her dishes, clothes, and body with the same country store soap. She changed jeans not too frequently and outgrew her only pair of good shoes while they were still in the white box that came from the mailman.

Still, the lady who ran the store that Joan reached by the pirogue boat made nice comments. And some people, the store lady said, who remembered Joan from years past when her grandfather came to the community parties, complimented her, "Now she must blossom." Joan did, with full cheeks that blushed the color of rose water lilies from new ideas and embarrassments. And Joan felt rare. These swamp flowers proliferated in the heat and the darkness, but Joan was the only young woman around.

Joan sat alone on the floor next to her grandfather's bed and tried to inhale deeply at the same time as him. At first, she thought this could help. But he didn't notice and it only served to make her feel more of his difficulty.

The first day her grandfather could not rise from bed, Joan went in the pirogue two hours away to the store where she called the doctor. They discussed taking her grandfather to the nearest city hospital. "We could make way to take him in the boat. But why suffer him?" the doctor said. "You a woman now." The doctor paused on the telephone for her to acknowledge his authority, "You got to take care of this, you. If he don't come around, if he go, you pack and you come stay by me."

Joan listened because her grandfather always said, "Go to the doctor house, if anything happen." Besides being her grandfather's friend, the doctor was the nearest advisor. The priest, sheriff, and schoolteacher all lived and worked close to each other in an area surrounded by high land. They clustered together to be convenient, they said. But that helped only people who got first to one of them.

Since the day Joan called the doctor, her grandfather lost his desire to talk and lay most of the time like a baby or how Joan imagined one to be. He slept off and on. When awake he stared ahead and his eyes filmed with water. Sometimes he drooled and wet on the bedcovers.

Joan felt he would die very soon, and she would bury him. She got pictures of herself in her mind, paddling the boat away from the burial. When she got those images, they often proved out.

Since a child, Joan saw clear pictures in her head during times of deep concentration. Sometimes, quicker than a picture a voice would give her advice. This voice too had the quality of predicting in advance something to happen. Once when she and her grandfather were hunting, the voice said, "Look over there." She saw a deer. Another time in the woods, the voice told her, "Stop." She just missed bumping into a snake hanging low on a branch.

Joan told her grandfather about these experiences. But he just advised she had good instincts, just like the animals knew a storm was coming, the birds from the North filled the ponds every winter, or the fish came close to the shore sunset and dawn. Joan had a special sense for nature, her grandfather said, and Joan agreed. She did not tell him that she knew in advance his words or requests for dinner. He might have thought her disrespectful.

Plus, the Bible assured Joan that all things were possible. Prophets saw visions. Demons took hold of people and had to be cast out. Joan felt safe and content in her special abilities. They helped her. They confirmed that her grandfather might soon be dead.

The old man called for Joan. She stood up and wiped her grandfather's face with a warm, damp cloth. His skin was thick and dry like an old piece of bark. His lips were parted and she could see the spittle collecting into one cheek. She lifted his head for a sip of water. But his face tilted to the side and the liquid spilled from his mouth like an overturned cup.

The woman at the store wanted Joan to live there, where she rowed every week for supplies. "You just a child," the woman behind the counter told Joan. "Yes, you could be a daughter to me?" But Joan shook her head no, and packed the canned food she bought into a small leather bag that she put over her shoulder. The dog waited on the dock of the store by the boat.

Joan did not know where to go. But just rowing away seemed a good start. She had taken her grandfather's body, wrapped in a sheet, out to the boat. He was light like a small animal. Joan closed the front door with the zipper of bent nails that held the screen flat when the wind was up from a rainstorm.

She took with her grandfather's body four empty half-gallon jugs that he kept for wine. He did not have too many around because he did not drink that often, only for special occasions. One remained half-full.

As she did for the more than a month of his sickness, actually for most of her life, she moved slowly and methodically. When her feelings welled up, she erased them. She had learned not to cringe when a rabbit needed to be skinned and gutted. She could watch with fascination alone when the heart of a turtle continued to pulse on the kitchen table. She had suspended her fear while her grandfather grew more sick, and she faced one new duty after another, cleaning up after him and waking to his gagging chokes in the night.

Joan was strong. Her grandfather once said her name came from the French saint set afire who went willingly into a war. So when he died, she buried him the way she knew. She rowed the boat out into the swamp, and she filled up the wine jugs with water by ducking them below the surface. Through the thumbhole for lifting the jugs she laced a rope and then tied it to her grandfather's body. Then she put them all overboard. The swamp folded her grandfather inside as he sank and she said prayers to remind herself his spirit left during the previous night, and now she submerged only his shell.

But Joan began crying and praying words from the Bible. And soon all jumbled around in her head, so that even the dog in the bow of the boat looked at her strangely. Her sobbing echoed on top of the water reaching far into the dark, empty spaces of swamp. And when she stopped, nature imitated her silence. But no longer did she feel its peace. Inside this timeless and changeless darkness, Joan felt different. She and the dog no longer belonged.

The doctor's house shone so white and brilliantly in the sun, Joan squinted. Back from the main road, the house was surrounded by grass, green and flat. Joan felt conscious of standing still when she stopped walking. Being on land that did not sink when her boot pressed into it made Joan feel strange. She did not need on this unfamiliar ground to shift her weight from one foot to the other, as near her home.

In her line of vision stood the big, square-shaped residence with its huge tapered yard and a white picket fence across the front. Joan didn't know anyone who lived like this. When younger, she took a bus ride and she saw these kinds of homes every few miles. But this time, she stood and looked without the impression of speed, or without shadow and trees framing her sight.

Joan felt dreamy. But she was unsure whether the fog in her head was due to the dream she had just entered or the dream she had just left. She knew only that her skull ached slightly and the hard sun made her sweat. Brightness surrounded her like an exaggeration of colors she saw the first moment she stood by the road.

She had waited there, not far from the supply store after leaving her boat at the dock. She walked a few miles up the oyster shell and gravel truck-path from the store to the highway.

The man who opened the door of the huge trailer truck asked her, "How much?" when she got on the cab seat. Joan did not understand, so she ignored him and gave him the address of the doctor's house. After a while, she told him about her grandfather.

She was just lucky, the truck driver said, that she got him and nobody else. How would she be safe?

"God bless you," she said good-bye when she got out.

"Mercy," the truck driver wiped his brow and wished her good luck.

Joan had felt during the ride a sensation coming from him, like sitting close to the fire. She ignored it because she felt uncomfortable. She did not want him to take pity on her. She was already afraid and only by staying quiet and keeping her distance could she not acknowledge it.

She could not see herself as he did. The man thought at first she was someone from the houses on Decatur or Bourbon Street in New Orleans who was stranded downriver. She wore such a strange outfit: the jeans and hat with animal skins laced around the band, leather bag and tall boots. She was beautiful. The plait she wore to her waist was the same color as her eyes, like rocks of tar set in a complexion of gold. But as soon as she got in the cab, he smelled the decay from the swamp. He had never picked up anyone like her.

If only she were a child, the doctor thought as he prepared to meet Joan, someone would perhaps adopt her. But physically she was a woman, although without the strength or the wit of the experience. Living anywhere outside of the swamp, she would be a victim. The modern world allowed no ignorance or indifference now on the part of participants. One moment of indecision and predators would see this girl's weakness. Then she could live the rest of her life with a wrong choice.

The transition from her quiet life would not be easy. Before he arrived almost a generation ago, the doctor remembered, he never wore shoes all day. Then, he owned two white shirts and one tie that he laundered by hand in the bathroom every night. He was expected to dress for classes in medical school. The other students laughed at him.

But he won out finally. He was accustomed to studying. Early in life, he read aloud at home. His habit became to repeat and explain to the younger children, and translate bills and letters for his mother who could not understand writing.

But the city boys, most of them monied, had as their hardest job to curb their good-time energy. Their college plans were to go out night after night. Fun did not play much part in the doctor's experience.

So many of the others did not graduate. But they returned to their rich families in uptown New Orleans and went insane like their weak fathers. Or they became drunks like their once beautiful Southern belle mothers who hungered for company.

Those medical students who did graduate now owned fine, expensive practices in the New Orleans districts where the streetcars ran. The doctor visited a colleague once in the city. This man charged fifty dollars to listen to perfectly strong old

ladies' hearts and to convince them of their lingering desirabil-
ity. At least this colleague spent one afternoon in the poor section
of town. He ministered from the back room of a drugstore to
people who really needed medical attention.

That day was more than an education, the doctor remembered. He felt better when he returned to his own rural community. He knew these people needed his knowledge. Still, his
situation often discouraged him.

These people could not afford the drugs he prescribed. So
while his costs rose greatly, he could not raise their fees. Most of
them would do without a doctor rather than pay more than ten
dollars for a visit. They depended on him to give them the
drugs, just like medicine men who once practiced in this part of
Louisiana. They expected lagniappe from the doctor, something
extra to go along with his services, as if he were a grocery store
clerk. Rarely did they treat him like a professional.

Maybe he could have achieved more success in New Orleans.
But then again, maybe not. The laughter of college boys still
rang in his ears. They made fun of him in school when he answered in half-French. His professors encouraged the ridicule,
"The state of Louisiana has been purchased, monsieur. Please
join us." He learned to speak good English once he used it every
day. But when he returned to the country, no one could understand him. So he began speaking as he did before he left to get
educated.

His city peers still lost no opportunity to demonstrate his un-
sophistication. On his last visit to a colleague, the rural doctor
complained about rising costs and expenses, and his patients' inability to pay. The city doctor said, "Look at the burden they are
to society now. Probably most of those you are treating were
mistakes anyway."

"Mistakes," the doctor said aloud when he left his colleague's
office and stepped into the too-bright New Orleans afternoon
sun. What a way for a healer to think about people.

But this girl who stood in his front room was one of those
kinds of "mistakes." He knew well about her. Born illegitimate
and then abandoned to her grandfather, she would get nowhere
in life. If she could get a job, she would be at best some kind of
servant. Her lack of skills, her isolation and unrealistic religious

beliefs gave the credentials for failure. The doctor just hoped that the state would not have to take care of her finally. For now, he would give her a home in exchange for odd jobs. Then she would have to leave, before his real live-in housekeeper got jealous.

The doctor wondered where in the future he could place this child. No matter his help, she would probably just run off like her mother and any number of other misfits to wind up in New Orleans. He thought the woman was there still. The old man died with that secret.

"Big thanks, Lejeune," the doctor said up to heaven. Now the responsibility was his of telling the girl her mother still lived. The old man became simply selfish or maybe he got afraid as he got older; the doctor understood that. "New Orleans she already got my one baby girl," the old man cried to the doctor in a time of weakness. He knew Lejeune just wanted to protect this next child. But the old man succeeded too well in his goal.

Here were the consequences. The child was ignorant and too stoic for a modern world. The doctor could see that just on his few visits. He could offer her few alternatives, even if she did have the sense to choose. Maybe he should send her off to a convent.

"Do they take illegitimate nuns?" he wondered. "Still, at that age, she will need the mother's approval." Her grandfather made the doctor swear not to tell the child that her mother remained alive. She left only to return to the city. "Better the girl think she got nobody than think they don't care, no?" the old man asked. The doctor agreed. But the old man ignored his part of the promise, to send her to school.

She spent only about four years learning to read and write with three other children in an unpainted frame house near the supply store.

The doctor once stood in the store as the woman who ran it tried to encourage Joan's grandfather to prepare her for the outside world. The woman wanted him to buy Joan a dress to wear to church festivals in town and for parties. She said, "Here, put your gal pretty in this here." The store owner pushed something lacy and bright yellow in front of the old man's face.

"What she go to use that for?" the old man replied in French.

"She traveling into the world at some time," the old lady, fat with the prosperity of trading flour and grease to country people for skins and fur, answered him in his own language.

"God got the time when to take care of that," he answered in English to make her understand how far he was from sharing her opinion. Then he pushed Joan by one shoulder toward the door.

But the doctor could see that Joan became first excited, then very disappointed. Before she left, the doctor handed her a bag of sugar ball candies in reparation.

"How you need that?" her grandfather told her to give them back. Joan wouldn't. Her grandfather said, "You'll see." He later told the doctor Joan ate the whole bag that night and got sick. Her grandfather said he just protected her from things "that got no place."

The doctor realized then he could do nothing as long as the old man lived. Now that she came to his doorstep, he wondered if he wasn't too late. His city colleague would say this kind of person did not need to be born. The pregnancy could have been corrected by science. She could have stayed innocent like an angel. The doctor thought of many others that his colleague would have no use for: Mrs. Labat who could not afford her pressure pills; Regaline who knew the weather on every date from the 1980s back through 1960, but who could not learn to spell; Thomas with the gimp leg that told the rain. Then the doctor thought, without them, he would have little variety in his work. Plus, he would not have them as friends. "Who can be so pragmatic?" the doctor thought. He would ask his city colleague who he would kill and who he would save. The doctor knew the answer already. His city colleague would discount most of his poor black patients immediately. But then, when the old white ladies died off, who would the city colleague have to treat, the doctor would point out. His colleague could not stand the idea of losing money.

The healing sciences were entrusted with the soul as well as the body, the doctor considered. He needed to give this girl Joan something to do. Room and board would be enough to start if she worked around the house. Maybe God sent her to him because he took care of the people who could not afford to pay. God did not want the doctor to be broke after all.

Joan awoke in the morning now to the smell of food and the feel of sunlight on her skin. She lay in bed and stretched her hand out and on the floor appeared a shadow. It moved just as she moved her hand, like an echo, except quicker and nearby. Joan was surprised to see shadow in daytime. She thought it only came on at night with the lamps.

Joan used the pitcher and jug on her dresser to wash up, although on her first day in the house Claudia, the housekeeper, bragged, "That's just for decoration. We got water running."

Claudia had walked Joan into the bathroom and showed her how turning the faucet chased the water down into the drain. Joan tried it again when she was alone. She turned it off and on seven times for good luck. No one could hear into the bathroom because the door shut tight like inside an icebox. It was cool and delicious in there. The tiles were so shiny and clean, Joan felt like licking them.

She told that to Claudia. But Claudia put her two hands to her face to hold the smile down in her mouth.

Joan saw the doctor did the same thing every time she called him to the "bird knock," the sound that whistled before someone came to the door. When she entered the "cold room" to dump the wastebasket, a person sat on a table wrapped in a sheet. He looked surprised. But Joan ignored him. When the doctor found out she had entered, he got very angry. "Don't you know how to announce yourself," his voice strained.

The next time, Joan opened the door, closed it behind her, and stood presenting the wastebasket at chest level. "I am Joan," she said. The doctor began laughing and the person on the table made a little scream and pulled the sheet up to her shoulders.

Joan felt like laughing too when she made them surprised and happy. But she did not want to be their joke. It made her feel like a small child again, ashamed in front of the adults.

She and her grandfather did the same things, Joan remembered as she dressed in the big bedroom alone. When he got up in the morning, he pushed to the wall the fabric curtain that separated their sleeping areas. Then they sat outside together for coffee. Some days they whittled pieces of bark on the porch or told stories. When his eyes hurt, she read to him. She did not feel that he looked after her any more than she looked after him. When he got older, in fact, he was the child as she told him what he could and could not do. Other times Joan spent walking in the woods or fishing with the dog in the pirogue.

Now she did not have the dog either. He was banished to the yard. Claudia would not let him in. "To have dog hair in this house?" she asked the doctor, and answered him too, "No." Joan suspected that Claudia did not even want Joan living inside.

Joan had stayed in the house for a week now, and for the first few days she had often heard, "It's her or me," coming from the front room. Then the doctor called Joan into the room to show her how to use something better or to tell her why to bring some item outside. The nutria rat that Joan caught near the thick part of the backyard and left in the kitchen was thrown into the garbage, even before Joan got to skin it. "Is good eating," she tried to tell Claudia. She did not even cover her mouth that time. Claudia screamed, "Ah!" and left the room. "Ah!" Joan knew now meant to leave Claudia alone. Claudia said, "Ah!" less lately. But when Joan entered a room, Claudia pulled her face tight to the middle like she expected "Ah!" to jump out and she was trying to hold it back.

Joan thought of her home in the swamp, her boat, the straight-backed chair where she read the Bible, and her very, very soft bed. She and her grandfather stuffed it with moss and bird feathers. Then he presented it to her as a gift for her thirteenth birthday. It was a grown person's size. She thought they were making it for him. She missed her grandfather.

They sang together in the evenings sometimes. He played the harmonica. She had a guitar. As a child he taught her a song: "Fait dodo Minette. Trois petites cochons du lait. Fait dodo ma petite bébé. Jusque l'age du quinze ans." She comforted herself now by going to sleep with that lullaby in her head.

Joan sang the song to the other children in the small school when she went. She had to leave when the teacher told her grandfather she had nothing more to teach Joan. She remembered their fight. The teacher wanted to send Joan to school in the city. She could come home on weekends like other young people did. Her grandfather said no.

"She got to go some time. She could live with the nuns in the week," the teacher argued.

Her grandfather said, "For what more she got to learn? Can't she read? The nuns to take care of her better than family?"

Joan concluded, as she overheard this conversation, that her grandfather outsmarted the teacher with too many questions. That too was the explanation he gave Joan. "She got no good answers for me," he said.

Finally, the teacher left them alone.

For a while, Joan wondered about the new school. Where would it be? What would it look like? One time, she day-dreamed a picture of the classroom into her head. Joan saw a square, white, frame house with extra rooms joined to the sides like wings. A dirt yard was adjacent, with a short flagpole. Joan saw small children in blue skirts or pants and white shirts lined up in front of the building. Then they marched inside. The hall-way was dark as they left the daylight. Joan appeared to be with them because she was temporarily blinded. The next picture she saw was inside a spacious room with many desks and oversized windows. All of the desks were filled except one.

After a while she stopped seeing the picture. And she also came to feel her grandfather right in his decision. Who could take care of her better than family? He devoted his life to raising her. Then she devoted herself to him.

Joan looked at herself in the mirror as she combed her hair. She was taller than she had imagined. She was solid and full. At sixteen, she could do just about anything a grown woman could. She compared herself to Claudia. Joan could keep house just as clean, maybe cleaner when she got on her hands and knees.

Joan could cook fresh and now frozen stiff that they took hard from the top part of the refrigerator. Joan could garden and plant. Her grandfather showed her good roots for tea that Joan found in the backyard.

But the more Joan helped out, the more Claudia seemed to get sad. Joan watched Claudia at the table with her head in her hands. Claudia would smoke a cigarette and shake her head sometimes and mumble. Joan could not tell what she said. Once, she heard Claudia say to the phone, "I know he paying her nothing. Some kind of way to get rid of me, huh?"

Claudia answered the voice on the other end, "What to fight? I'm old now. She young."

Joan felt proud at first, "Yes, I'm young." Later, she did not know whether that was a fault or a compliment.

"I'm getting too old and useless, ain't I child," her grandfather would sometimes ask Joan. At those times, she felt useless for being young. She had no answer. If she was happy about herself and her age, it would be painful to him. "I wish I was old too," she would say in response. She came to believe it. She wished she was old now so she would not have to be in the care of others and also because her grandfather in his age had some place to go. She did not.

Joan decided to lay back on the bed. She lingered long enough to follow the sun's rays with her hand as they moved across the floor.

The doctor came to the door first, "You sick, Joan?" He called her Joan with an accent that sounded soft and concerned. She was dressed so she went to the door. "No, sir. Non, m'sieur."

"But why then you still in the bed?" He continued to speak in the familiar tone in patois. She had many answers. But they congealed in her throat full of emotion. "Pas raison," she told the doctor. "Today, I work in the yard."

But there were no jobs outside. So for most of the day, Joan sat far back in the lot. The dog came up to her. He nuzzled against her calf. He smelled different since they left the swamp. This too was because of Claudia, although he did not want to adjust to his cleanliness. After his bath he ran into a nearby field and rubbed back into the mud. He ran one shoulder to the ground first then the other. Then he rolled on his back and kicked his feet up into the air.

That day, Claudia rolled her eyes over to Joan. Claudia liked to show that she knew better than Joan, and was more of a grown woman. But it was not Joan's fault what the dog did. So she shrugged and looked away. But Joan resolved to begin smelling sweet like the soap, even if the aroma was strange to her.

Now, Claudia called Joan from the back door. Claudia was silhouetted in front of the kitchen light. The sun was going down. Claudia went inside for a while. She came again to the door, this time accompanied by the doctor. "Joan. Joan," he hollered. But Joan continued to sit under the tree far back in the yard. When she didn't answer, she could see their heads bowed toward one another, talking.

Joan did not want to answer because she was confused. The wrong time to appear seemed to be when they called. What explanation would she give for hiding in the yard? Suddenly, she felt lonelier than ever with her grandfather, although more people were with her.

"But they're not my family," she cried to herself. "I have no family, anymore, anywhere." And with that thought, she stayed outside in the back lot, more comforted by nature than even the clean bathroom. When Claudia found her outside the next morning, she called her "a little pig." Those words were the same as her grandfather sang lovingly, "petite cochon," but said now in anger.

"We looked for you all night, Joan. Why you don't came here?" the doctor said. But Joan could think of nothing to say. He looked as if he wanted to be angry, but his eyes did not cooperate. She felt they really wanted to know.

But Joan was not sure how to tell him her feelings. She wanted to go back into the swamp. In his house, she felt lonely and strange. She felt more like a child with them taking care of her and she didn't like it.

"I'm sorry to do wrong, sir," she said.

Joan looked around at the room that the doctor called "study." It was darker than the rest of the house, and so more comfortable for her. Joan thought the doctor liked it better in here too. Often she heard him reading aloud or making comments to himself alone in the evenings. Books filled many shelves and wood covered the walls. They were the same dark silvery color the swamp trees took at a particular time before sundown.

Joan felt the doctor watching her. He touched her shoulder so she had to return his look.

"What to do with you, Joan, if you don't like it here?"

"I miss to have family," were her only words.

The doctor left Joan alone in the room and sitting in a big, green leather armchair after he told her, "Your mother could be alive." Joan felt at first he was playing some terrible meanness on her, perhaps for making him worry all night, like sometimes her grandfather pulled the dog by one leg to get him out of the house when Joan's cajoling wouldn't work. Seeing the dog hopping on three legs and giving pleading howls and hearing Joan say, "Leave him; leave him alone," seemed to satisfy some feeling in her grandfather.

Joan took that sense as one they did not share. She was never tempted to be that kind of mean. Sometimes she neglected her plants in the pots until they shriveled up. But she never desired to hurt something breathing. When she hunted she made sure her animals were quickly dead. She even gutted and cleaned the fish as soon as she caught them.

Now she had to consider, it could be true that her mother still lived. Joan sat in the chair and wondered, had a miracle happened? Having a mother was God's answer to Joan? "Holy Mary," Joan got on her knees, "I'll live with my mother. She could take care of me and be with me. And everything will be all right."

Joan bowed her head to consider and pray. For her the room became dark. Her eyes pulsed behind the red lids even though she tried to still them like something alive she did not want to acknowledge. Her voice said, "If your mother is living, she will just die again." But Joan could not picture her mother's death. Instead she saw herself feeling surrounded by thunderstorms. She could not make out the room. But she heard the rain heavy and hissing outside like a nest of snakes. And she heard the slamming of voices against a wall. They were like wails and negations. "No." "Stop." "Oh no." Joan's own voice was saying, "I don't want to go there." Then she felt a warm wind like a Sunday breeze when she was peaceful and sitting alone on the porch. It felt soft across her forehead like a passing hand or secure like a sucking thumb.

Joan pressed her fingers to her eyelids. It caused her picture to dim. Only her breathing resounded loud in the silence of the empty room. Her thoughts continued with a logic that Joan did not want to own.

If she was the kind of mother Joan wanted in childhood, Joan would not have to seek her. "She would be here," Joan thought. She wouldn't have had to bury her grandfather alone. She wouldn't be wondering about her future. She would have a place to be and someone with whom she belonged. Was it better to have no mother or a mother she never saw? God was invisible. But He had a reason and the power to make such a choice.

"What is Your will," Joan prayed to bring her feelings to some resolution. If she saw her mother, Joan thought, she would say, "I am a woman now too. Is there anything you can tell me?" Joan imagined herself speaking boldly and cruelly to this parent, although she really needed an answer.

"When I meet her, this is what I will tell her." Joan picked at the nails that held the green leather to the wood of the chair. The bones of Joan's fingers made a little vibration in the bones of the furniture, even though in between the wood and the leather were soft fabrics and cushions layered for reasons to stop such reverberations from happening.

"I do want to find her," Joan told the doctor when she left the study. But she pretended to be more sure than she was. "We will live together soon. I can't wait." Inside, Joan wondered still as she did in the swamp. Would she be able again to erase this mother, as necessary, out of her thoughts?

The doctor had not been in New Orleans since the last visit to his colleague. Now, he, Claudia, and Joan drove in the car. On the backseat was an ice cooler, blankets, and food that Claudia packed. Joan's cowboy hat sat in the back window.

It was not a grim task. The doctor saw the girl's desire for her parent growing, although he did expect more happiness in her initial reaction.

He tempered his offer that they seek out Joan's mother. "Maybe she's in New Orleans. But I don't know. We don't know who she is now, or where she is, or if she ready to take care of a child, I got to say it," the doctor stared at the girl when he saw her confused reaction. He thought he knew about the maternal bond. It was always existent. It stretched over time and even beyond death and living. People still prayed to their dead mothers in heaven, placed flowers on their graves every week, and carried their photographs, the doctor knew, in the town where he was born.

The mothers too kept the birth of each child as special, no matter how many. In the doctor's family were nine. How women changed these times of pain into pleasure, the doctor still wondered, although he did not dispute it. He assisted at plenty births, some of them terrible. Sometimes the women struggled for hours. And after it was over, a month or two later, they couldn't even remember how much they hurt or they translated the pain as unimportant. "Look at my beautiful boy," one woman whom he saw suffer the worst said, "and tell me how can I remember anything but God's gifts."

He hesitated then to tell her the child appeared slow, even at that young age. He waited until the third examination and took several tests before he suggested the child might be retarded. And then, how did she respond? First she appeared sad and then she said, "How my life will be full always teaching him." The doctor became speechless.

That day, he cursed God for giving a child so unworthy to this woman who was so beautiful and strong. She would not, in her old age, be taken care of by her son. In fact, for most of her days she would serve him. What justice was there to that? The doctor could not sleep at night, thinking about the plagues of the world and how God allowed it.

Later he realized one reason such experiences so frightened and confused him. He worried sometimes that he was spared. Why wasn't life that bad for him? Didn't he come from a poor family? Why did he achieve? Why were his brothers and sisters so healthy and smart and self-sufficient? And then, was self-sufficiency the most a person could ask out of life anyway? After the basics, what was there? For him, the goal had been recognition. But then he found out in medical school that the monied city boys would do the most research because they had connections to those scholarships.

The doctor had gotten far enough by just attending. At least, that's how he rationalized. He had passed into the white medical school without anyone finding out he was colored, as people called blacks in those days.

The doctor's own family came from a place not far from

where he now lived. Typical of the region, he could not locate his ancestors too far back. But he knew enough to acknowledge there were Africans, Indians, and French among them.

His admission forms were altered for entrance by another black in the same situation. This school official passed too. His pleasure was to sneak into this public medical school any of their number. It was his small stab to disturb the lies that held white purity as the only intellectual standard in the region. He didn't bother that some of these students continued on in life as white. That was their failure of conscience or politics. Others returned to their nearby black communities with the needed skills and education that passing afforded them.

The doctor was part of the latter group. He went back to a very poor town where race was an issue far behind eating and living. The people in Sagetville did not discriminate for one major reason. If someone did try to consider himself better because of a particular color or shade, he would be reminded by others of his dark grandmother who was a saint and his white grandfather who was an alcoholic, or vice versa.

Plus, only in cities was race important because it determined economics into the next generation. Unlike rural areas, where almost everyone had an individual or family enterprise—trapping, farming, or fishing—and were all on the edge of subsistence, in the cities, blacks, and everyone else, worked for institutions. The doctor heard the institutions were even larger and harder to enter up in the North. It was the place to go during his time for more freedom, people said. But the doctor heard stories of poor people freezing to death. So neither the weather nor attitudes of other states beckoned him.

Because his appearance gave few clues to his race, his patois usually first caught attention. And as an additional discrimination, many people thought he was rural and uneducated when they heard him. So because of his race, his country roots, and his arrogance to be visibly proud on all counts, the doctor kept himself apart from most people. Too many only wanted to start trouble with him. He felt his solitude kept others' bitterness out of his heart, and it allowed him to find the most efficient ways to progress. Now, he could be as he was without apology. From the whites, he desired nothing.

He, Joan, and Claudia stayed in an apartment that one of his colleagues offered for their visit to New Orleans. "You can have it, my extra place. Besides I'm flying to the islands this fall," he bragged. The doctor hadn't expected to get a place to stay so easily. He had planned to call many physicians. He did not mind imposing on some of these people. In fact, he got a certain pleasure in showing up from time to time.

That was because some of those men who came from his same background became pretentious. They spoke to him plainly enough when they were alone, sometimes even in dialect. But if another entered the room, their accents changed so that their ancestors could not be located.

"La-bas?" he loudly asked one acquaintance who changed his own character after another person entered the room. The doctor reached for the door handle to leave. The questions, "there?" and "the bottom?" referred simultaneously to the means of the doctor's exit, to the reason for his departure because of his associate's changed attitude, and to the place they all grew up. The innuendo was so well understood, it was ignored completely by the doctor's colleague. He still hid when it was no longer a necessity, the doctor resented.

Now, the doctor saw how New Orleans had changed. When he, Claudia, and Joan arrived at the concierge, they did not get a second glance although they were all black. They demonstrated their race in its variety with skin the color of pecans, porcelain, and gold. One had hazel eyes, another black, the third brown. And their hair was singularly straight, kinky, and subject to fall somewhere in between depending on the day's humidity. The doctor saw as much variation in many Louisiana families.

Joan tried to study the face of every person as the car arrived on the streets of New Orleans. But too many people blurred past the windows, just like the trees flew sideways on the road.

Joan wanted to control her anxious feeling at moving so quickly. Claudia and the doctor had helped Joan practice for the car ride while they ran errands, like people in the city let their dogs jump into the backseat.

At first Joan felt similar to a bewildered animal. She was completely alert and moved her head often toward sounds on the side and behind her. It was a wonder, she heard Claudia and the doctor say to one another, that Joan didn't stay dizzy from this continual turning. Joan overheard and took these words and other of their directions. So she tried to "relax," "calm down," and "talk slow" at the right times while at others she learned to "sit up straight," "pay attention," and "come right here" as they told her.

New Orleans was more than she imagined. It had so many different faces. She could not remember one past seeing the last.

How did people recognize each other among so many? It was different for animals. They acted on smell. Joan recognized them too. The raccoons near her home in the swamp who came from the same mother had a particular grey strip of hair on the same side. The supply store woman's pony had a diamond on its muzzle, like the mare.

Now for the first time Joan wondered, when people saw her, what did they think? She now considered if she resembled her mother. But what was that like? Did she inherit her height, her eyes, or her temper? Animals possessed emotional compositions too. Some dispersed a mean spirit throughout the litter. Others kept a skittish streak from generation to generation.

Joan tried to picture her mother. But she could only imagine a girl about the same age as herself. In this frame, the girl sat on the porch of Joan's house. Her chin rested in the palm of her right hand and she looked down into the water. Joan could not see her face and had taken that position many times herself. Perhaps she was just remembering the solitude and even the loneliness she felt sometimes in the swamp when her grandfather left in the boat to go hunting or fishing. She and the dog waited then feeling empty and fearful. There was always the chance that he would not return.

Her grandfather was gone now forever. She missed him badly. He taught her to balance the pirogue through the most thin and twisted swamp alleys. Her grandfather taught Joan direction and advised her that the largest and best body of water in the United States lay at the foot of the Mississippi River.

Joan saw it as a huge clearing emerging from an overhang of

trees. In her mind, she paddled her boat down the wide river and entered the Gulf. She thought the water was as deep as cypress were tall. Fish hurtled themselves over the bow of her boat. The air smelled of rain, salt, and deer. Although the Gulf was huge, it had a shoreline in her picture to the right and left. She could not understand the Gulf's crystal blue water or its deceptive depth caused by the sunlight. For one reason, her grandfather had told Joan only some information, and some of it was wrong.

Joan's special intuitive sense operated in this odd manner. Her pictures were more accurate if she based them on truth or if she knew nothing at all. When someone gave Joan the wrong facts, she trusted them strongly and her imagination was obliterated by her faith.

At the same time she missed her grandfather, she felt disgust that he kept her mother a secret for so long. She felt angry in a way she could not completely understand. She never felt this emotion so intensely before. She would get mad at the dog for turning the garbage or even, when she reached her teens, at her grandfather for some comment. But the anger did not gnaw her stomach as this feeling did and come up into her throat in the night so that she dreamed about faceless problems and innumerable little meanings of words like orphan, daughter, family, children.

They would enter her dreams first like distant returning echoes on water that would then stretch out visibly like a phrase on a blackboard. They became nightmarish as they grew louder and bigger like something a person in school tried to repeat to you until you understood them. But she couldn't. Joan only remembered her school days lasting a few years before her grandfather decided that was enough. So she found no connection beyond her grandfather's assertion that her mother was dead and now the information reversed.

But coming to New Orleans, Joan discovered more of her reasoning and her intelligence. She was able to read the maps and street signs. There were not many words she did not know since she had learned to read the Bible, but now the words had new meanings. The differences between the secular and religious confused Joan at first. "Don't walk" did not mean "do not follow a path for fear of reprisal." It simply meant to wait before crossing the street. It made Joan think this city life was very easy and far from the spiritual, truer meanings of living.

The doctor was handed a photocopy of Joan's birth certificate in New Orleans City Hall almost immediately after his request. The speed was unlike his experience in the small, country towns. There, he waited while clerks printed the information by hand or promised to mail it to him in a week.

In New Orleans, the effort was almost too quick and casual considering the importance of the facts these papers contained. This big, faded green office with a few scattered old wooden tables and its nervous fluorescent light held the recordings of crucial events for countless living beings.

The doctor tried to imagine all the humanity embodied in this office. He delivered many babies and never ceased to be amazed about the progression from conception to personality. He knew life was really a gift. Man could never invent it. There was a Creator as far as the doctor understood. No matter how much flesh the doctor stitched together or heartbeats he revived, he could never lay claim to making one human.

And death was a similar mystery. He saw the breath leave a number of people and never did he have any feeling but sadness, an empathy deep like a response from his own soul. Early in his career when he answered calls at Angola prison, he talked to men on death row. Some claimed to have been happy to kill their victims. "He deserved it," each justified the behavior. But later the man would whisper, "But I'm sorry it had to be me." Even the most evil prisoner that the doctor met, a man called Snake by the others, confessed regret.

"I felt like a child watching the air come out of a balloon. I wanted him to come back, to bust up alive and fight like a man. But he died right in front of me and I felt the worst. I didn't want that feeling from my hands. He deserved to be hit harder from what he said to me. But I hurt right behind it, feeling bad since after he's dead."

The doctor restrained himself from telling this man that when killing life, he took the biggest creative gift of God and through mortal pride destroyed His prerogative. That has got to be a bad feeling, the doctor could have said or he could have reminded the prisoner that the devil was acting through him. Instead, the doctor suggested to Snake that he talk to someone in the clergy, maybe to confess. But Snake puffed up his wide chest to return to the attitude he had when the doctor entered the room. "What you think I just did? I ain't telling nobody. Who you think you are anyway?" he said. The guard who stood nearby jerked the chains around Snake's ankles when his voice raised. The guard said, "Don't believe not a thing that one says, Doc. He ain't got no respect for nobody."

Where did all the people go when they died, the doctor wondered. Where did they live on earth? All those people in the City Hall files, where were they born? The doctor thought of all the strange places he assisted mothers panting and sweating—taxicabs, hospital beds, bedrooms, and bars.

According to Joan's birth certificate, attending her birth was one Irene Campland. The event took place in a house low in the ninth ward almost to Plaquemines Parish and out of the city. The doctor decided to drive to the address on the birth certificate to see if Campland still lived there and ask her about the mother named on the form: a Miss Oceola Leontine.

As the doctor walked to get his car near the French Quarter apartment, he decided to stop in a bar. He saw as he strolled that Bourbon Street had changed little since he was there last. Now the advertisements showed more skin and expressed more sexual diversity. But the same intent remained.

Inside the bar was the same as well; permanent darkness existed. A smell that probably had never left since the Second World War of liquor, stale cigarettes, and urine clung to the room. The doctor could not see the label on the bottle that filled his shot of scotch. But, the doctor remembered, that was the point.

He did not see either the face of the woman who appeared quickly and soundlessly next to him. She asked for a drink too. B-drinkers, they called these women in his time. And just like then, the bartender filled her glass with colored water while charging the doctor for alcohol.

He knew it was illegal. But here was another generation prac-
ticing the same tricks. People always seemed ready to fill the
glasses as well as the criminal ranks.

This woman's voice showed her to be very young. So did her
opinions. She liked "heavy" music. She did not believe in elections. She was "friends" with her parents, although they did not
know her telephone number. "I call them up and let them know
I'm OK. Long as they're OK, it's all right," she said.

The doctor asked if she ever considered working a job a little
bit "better." She looked at him directly and said softly, "Honey,
what did you have in mind?" Then she laughed, "Oh, you're
serious. This is a good job. What else to do? I stay out of trouble
and I get home before night." Then she asked the doctor for spe-
cific pills—Valium, Prednisone or diazepam. She thought he
could "at least do one favor."

"I don't think it would mix with the alcohol," the doctor
responded.

"Aw, this isn't . . . ," she started to call out to him as he rose
and walked toward the door. But the bartender banged the heel
of his hand on the counter near where she sat. "Oh, come back,"
she now laughed, cheerful and desperate. "Let's have more
fun," she pleaded louder as the doctor exited.

The sun was blinding. It was just afternoon. Stepping inside
that bar was like a nightmare. What pleasure had he discovered in
it when he was young? Partly, he was included in the carousing.

How quiet his life now was compared to this side of New Orleans. And Joan's home in the swamp was archaic. Visiting her
house with the grandfather was like returning into some primitive century, some prehistoric time. The darkness and the rigid-
ity of the home fixed in place, pressed in by constant isolation.
When trees fell in that part of the swamp, no one but Joan and
her grandfather heard the sound. But the doctor considered,
somewhere a ripple of water hit the river and Gulf shores just a
little harder.

Almost all day while the doctor was gone from the apartment,
Joan stood on the balcony wondering about the varieties of
women who passed on the sidewalks below. Where did she fit

among them? Some wore their hair loose and curly. From her vantage, their bare shoulders jutted square out of blouses where sleeves should go.

Joan's hair swelled up from the humidity. But instead of plaiting it Indian style on each side of her head and joining the plaits at the back as was her habit, she pulled it straight back into a rubber band as she would have early in the morning before she had time to comb.

"I see a change in our girl already," the doctor commented.

"She better not go too fast, no," said the housekeeper.

"I'm all right." Joan glanced again toward the street. The other women she saw wore dresses a lot. The ones who wore jeans, like she did, had on beautiful lacy shirts, bare sandals, or high heels. Joan was glad the apartment was just one story up, so she could study the women as they approached. She did not miss the men either. So many kinds! There were lots who appeared close to her age.

One of them, as he passed, even looked back up at her. "Hello, beautiful," he whistled.

She whistled back. Like the mockingbird she heard often in the forest, she copied the sound sliding up the scale and then quicker back down. He laughed, waved, and kept going. Then she whistled "Bob-white, bob-white," just like the little birds she knew. This time, when he waved he was no longer looking at her. She went "Caw-caw-caw" like the crows, "caw-caw-caw." But he was a half-block off and other people stood below her balcony looking up at her.

"Throw me something, sister," one of them rattled his hands high above his head as if seeking a present like the ones thrown to street people at carnival time. Joan ran inside and returned near the balcony only to latch the glass doors.

"Is too hot for you, huh?" Claudia thought Joan was escaping the sun into the air conditioning. "Is a lot different for a girl such as yourself," Claudia continued. "I know you got no mother yet so to speak of . . ."

John interruption, "But I will."

". . . but seem if you need anybody, sometime, I could be just as as good as them. You listening?" Claudia tapped Joan on the knee.

"But I'll find my mother and I'll go to live in her house," Joan insisted.

"Till then, don't throw out what I say, no," Claudia rose and touched Joan's right shoulder.

If the doctor could not find her mother, Joan had a plan. "God provide. He provide for the birds of the air, don't he," she said quietly. She did not want to depend and impose on others who were not family. Her grandfather taught her to be too proud. She could take care of herself alone if necessary. She was only confused now because of too much activity.

New Orleans was so different from the swamp where precious silence allowed her to concentrate. It was peaceful there and Joan had many tasks—quilting, reading her Bible, cooking, washing, cleaning. In the city, there was nothing for her to do. She just worried most of the day. When would they find her mother? How would she act? Would she really accept Joan? "What if she don't like the way I look," the young girl watched herself in the mirror.

She was nothing like the girls on the sidewalk, Joan thought. She was thin and repulsive. She was plain. All of her clothes covered all of her. "What if I'm too stupid for her? I got no city in me," Joan thought as she framed the ponytail around her face. "Is all a mistake," she regretted her existence.

Night was beginning to fall in the French Quarter. Lights made small faded universes at each corner.

Joan looked through the window to the dim darkness outside. She knew the sky could get so much blacker, clear and positive. There was a particular spot on the porch in the swamp that jutted far over the water where the cypress trees and their moss did not block her view. She could see straight up. That was her space, a triangle of nothing bounded by stars into the shape a child draws a house. "Look, Papa, voici cote' moin habite. Ici moin re'te," she told him, here is where she lived.

Suddenly, she wanted to see it, the deep black darkness, the vast space between the cypresses, the clear lane to heaven. She went to the balcony. But looking up, she could not see far. She viewed only the tin floor of the second story balcony and the wooden trestles that held it up. To see past, she leaned back over the railing. She wasn't thinking of the ground below or how for a moment she was suspended in air except for two points where the small of her back touched the balustrade and her toes balanced her weight off the ground.

"Joan, you crazy. You trying to break your neck, kill yourself?" Claudia rushed over and pulled Joan by the hand into the house.

Joan began weeping and could not stop. And she could not recall just one reason. Many confusing thoughts came at the same time. She wondered why grandfather, her mother, her dog, her house on the bayou, and her heaven were all gone from her now. Even if she returned to the swamp, all would be sadly different.

In the Faubourg Marigny across Esplanade Street from the French Quarter, Oceola Leontine lived this year. She was currently a redhead. More often she was a brunette with coppery streaks of hair that she called "blonde." On the nights that she wasn't too hung over or depressed, she walked into the Quarter to make her living.

"She was a beautiful baby," she thought about her daughter when she entertained new friends in the local bars with the infant picture. It showed a dark-haired newborn whose putty face had changed greatly in the intervening sixteen years, but Oceola did not know it. Oceola told people the child was born two years previously. "With her father," Oceola told those who asked whereabouts. Most of the time, no one was that curious.

The photo served as a screen for Oceola, an appropriate drama she acted out with new men. If they showed sympathy, she felt safe enough to take them where they paid the hotel.

With this type, she was more comfortable. Then she could drink and complain about her situation, a reality she did little to change. Instead, she hoped it would change itself if she were particular. Many girls just took the highest price. They were strictly business. Oceola felt herself open for the possibility of love.

Also, her logic was, if she took the man who bragged about having the most money, he intended to keep it. It was too much work to get that kind to loosen up.

Oceola's type showed her a picture of his children too. So they began with soft things in common. Their similarity, however, was not that they were parents. They discussed that "just now," "right at this time," they were in a bad state that companionship could probably fix. On the inside, they felt they would forever hurt.

Oceola did not intend to spend her life like this. But after New Orleans she could not go back to that swamp. She spent too many years with that old man, a tyrant, she explained to her old and new friends. He planned to marry her to one of his fools, one of those trappers or hunters who smelled bad all the time, and didn't have an easy hand with a woman.

And didn't she know now that those country bumpkins went straight to the houses like everyone else when they came to New Orleans? It made no difference that they were religious. In fact, it gave them something good to confess, Oceola joked to the other girls who drank together frequently to celebrate their own madness.

Nobody, including herself, wanted to be like she was, Oceola would say, "But who got a choice?"

Women, unlike the working men who patronized them, could not get jobs in construction, make cash trading stock in the business district, do cement finishing, or trap animals for a living. Women who tried union jobs on the dock were hounded until they left. And the factories hired only a few people of either sex at a time.

Let the women's righters say what they wanted, these women agreed, first of all, good work "ain't."

Of course, occupations existed other than prostitution. They could clean houses or mop floors in the downtown buildings. But Oceola and her friends had contorted their pride so that they felt keenly the diminished respect laborers got from the public. Like Oceola, the other women would not defend a righteousness in their job. But they felt, considering the attention received by them or the houseworkers, they got more of it. Women who broke their backs dumping trash cans and washing lavatories never got a wink when they walked through the corridors of the French Quarter hotels.

Besides, Oceola bragged to all, she learned quickly the tricks of dressing and walking. So easy. She was willing to instruct anyone: "Men are so primitive, so dumb, so basic." All men considered in their dealings with women were crotch and commerce, she believed. She, on the other hand, thought deeply. She often considered hell as her present and afterlife.

The doctor woke up kind of foggy, thinking all sorts of unrelated ideas. The young woman who approached him in the bar appeared in his dream like a galloping pony with a white diamond-shaped space on its forehead. Then he seemed to be in the swamp. He was so hot and sweaty. Then he was transported to forty years ago, into an old-fashioned bathtub with a woman. Then he was outside of it while she remained in. She was beautiful, soaping her body under the bubbles that stayed on the water's surface. Then she lowered her head to soap her face. When she lifted it, the bubbles remained, covering her features. The doctor waited for her to rinse. But she didn't. In a sort of innocent way, she waited for him to. That's when he woke up. He was waiting for her. She was waiting for him.

The doctor thought maybe the dream was the effect of cheap scotch. He knew half a day would pass before that poison would burn through his system. He decided to call Irene Campland first.

"I never seen her in many years. But I remember all about her still, yes," the old lady answered on the telephone. "Nice as I was too. Not a hello, dog," she continued.

The doctor, in one of the old lady's rare pauses, took liberty to invite himself over.

"It's my house," she said in the affirmative, a visit was fine with her.

When he arrived, he had to shout from the front gate for her to hold back the dogs in the yard. There were signs all around, misspelled and handwritten, and tied by wire coat hangers to the gate. "Keep Aout!" "Badog," had an S dangling below in another color like a fallen off puppy. "None your business," she pointed out for him. "I put that for those people all the time asking me 'who live here?' I say, 'What is it your business?' Want to know my name. Want to be calling me up on the phone. Want to buy property. Buy property. I say, 'How much?' They say, 'Can't tell.' I say, 'Get on 'way from here if I don't shoot you. Quick!'

"Now I think they just wait for me to die. That's all right. I'm not afraid of no spirits. I got enough of them. Bad and good," she talked continuously.

The doctor did not wonder why Irene Campland let him visit her after her next question. "How much you give me to tell?" she broke his guard with stares from two bloodshot eyes.

"About what?" he stalled.

"I don't mind dying and taking you with me," she answered. "First, the girl owe me money anyhow."

The doctor peeled off twenty dollars. She leaned into his wallet when his head was down.

"Fifty." She pushed the top of her body forward like a broken board. The heels of her hands were on her knees, which were spread wide apart over her misshapen and slippered feet.

The doctor thought of the dogs loose in the yard again and the long trip he'd taken. "Here," he frowned at the old lady in the chair opposite where he stood.

She motioned to a straight-backed wooden chair like a schoolteacher's, "No need for you to make yourself comfortable. You not staying that long."

The old lady began about Oceola. "She was so stupid when she come to me. Big like this." The old woman put her hands out to indicate pregnancy.

The doctor thought that motion ironic on such a skinny old woman.

"I say, 'Girl, why you wait so long?' She still act like she not made up her mind," the old lady was frowning as she told the story. She took the butt of a small cigar out of her ashtray and lit it. "Her friend tell me, 'She religious.'

"'Well, she liable go to hell anyway,' I tell them, 'for what she done done.' Then this girl, she start to crying. Her friend, the man she was with, then he couldn't take it. 'Shut up,' he say. 'Didn't I tell you to shut up?'

"I ain't ascared of hell," the old lady blew out a puff of smoke. "I seen worse misery on earth. And that's what I tell her right then. And the boyfriend, that's what I think he was anyhow, he laugh, 'See, we got somebody here not even afraid of the devil. So what you crying for?' And the girl quieted up. I think she was mostly afraid of him. 'And I'm afraid of being poor,' I try to make her a joke. But she wasn't going that far. So I just ask for my money, 'In advance,' I tell all of them."

Most rural midwives had more compassion, the doctor thought. Money was not even the issue with the ones he knew. They were happy to bring healthy babies into the world. He remembered the woman who helped his mother on many occasions. Mrs. Amy, he thought, was her name. The way people said it, it sounded like Mrs. Aimez, Mrs. Love in French. He actually wasn't sure that was not the spelling. But she was "American." In their town, that meant Protestant.

Mrs. Amy inspired him early to medicine. "There is nothing better on earth than to bring new life into this world. Yes, people may say, 'It's too harsh. We can't afford it. That baby might be ugly.'" They both laughed. "But Ugly might invent a drug for sickness or build a town hall. Besides he looks like his daddy, I say." The doctor never saw Mrs. Amy take a dollar. They just made sure she always had enough eggs and preserves. She often said to everyone in the room when she entered their home, "First, I thank you very kindly for everything."

This woman who sat across from the doctor was not like Mrs. Amy. Her tobacco-stained teeth jutted sparse like claws out of a fish mouth. Her face was cold, and so were her pointed eyes set in that pale, waxed-paper skin. It was as if she were the devil, and that's why she was not afraid. She could have been dead already and taken form just for his visit. The doctor scared himself with his own imagination. He was an intelligent man, he reminded his fear. But it was a very basic emotion.

Once when he was very young, he heard that a child died not far from his house. This boy had been murdered, the talk around the rural community held. A stranger strangled him, people said. And they were helpless to solve the crime because everyone nearby knew each other. It was surely someone passing through, they insisted, not one of them. The sadness and inability to help the boy's family set a gloom through all community activities. People got teary-eyed upon meeting each other at market when they saw his relatives. The doctor, a boy about that age too, was told often to take many precautions. For a long time, he could go nowhere alone. But at night he dreamed he was being chased by the devil. He often woke up screaming. His mother sat by his bedside and his older brothers and sisters took turns. But they all told him the same thing, "If it's the devil, pray to God. He is more powerful."

For a while when he was teenaged and rebellious, the doctor considered his faith merely superstition. But when he got older and realized, yes, he was vulnerable, yes, he would die, he was not eternal, the doctor found a spiritual power like God as a comforting thought. Whether his belief contained a large measure of fear or superstition no longer seemed very important.

Now, he found himself saying a prayer for courage to look into the old lady's eyes. He saw nothing but hardness, no demarcation of iris. Seemingly she kept the warmth of humanity out of them by sheer concentration. She was talking now excitedly.

"I put the cloth on her face and I say, 'Here, drink this whisky.' But she shake her head no. I say, 'Here, girl. Don't be fool enough to chance your own life.' Then before I know it she jump up, run out the bathroom. Is naked. Running out the front door. She made me so angry. I called her everything. Some people on the block let her into their house. But a few months later I'm still the one he call to birth it. I didn't give her no whisky then for real." The old lady sat back in her chair and stared out into her empty room, satisfied with the punishment.

The doctor wanted to punch her. Not often was he impelled to violence. But his revulsion came out. Evil should be handled on its same terms. That was the reality of life beyond its sweetness. Some people should have been stopped before they hurt others. He was looking at one of them.

He could not think of another question to ask. He had learned more than he wanted to know. Evil was not a new invention and being born ugly was better than anything this old lady had planned for children.

"Benitez-nous, Monsieur," was all he could mumble. They were the first words he said before accepting his plate three times a day, "Bless us, Lord."

"The daughter wants to see the mother," he finally said.

"I want to see her too. She still owe me." The woman looked

up at him. The doctor was standing. He opened the door himself
and went out. Whatever the scent he carried as he left that house
in such anger and shame, the dogs stayed away from him.

Another old lady was standing outside on a nearby porch
when he left the house. She waved hello in a shy way. But when
she saw the look on his face, she called him over more urgently.
"Here," she said. "Give her whatever you got to pay for that
property. Just get her away from around us."

"I don't want to buy her land," the doctor replied.

"It's been too long. Too long I heard those children crying. In
the night, when I'm sleeping I hear babies, 'Mama, mama,
mother.' Little ones' voices. They say she got the bones buried in
her yard."

"Oh, no," the doctor started to back away.

"I'm a religious woman and I stay here, just because of that,"
the neighbor continued. "If I can stop any of them, any young
girls before they go into that house, I have done the good work."
She looked at him squarely in the face and the doctor saw truth.

"You wouldn't happen to remember, maybe sixteen years
ago, a girl running out of there naked?" the doctor ventured.

"Yes, praise God. That was a strange sight. He come and get
her from me a couple days later. But I told her not to go. She was
just weak for him. Man named Aces. Until she got pregnant,
they was Aces and O.C. down at the Peacock," she pointed in
the direction of a local tavern.

Oceola Leontine was O.C. to the men who whistled, amened,
and applauded each of her Friday performances at the Blue Peacock. That could have meant her talent was special. But this bar
was only one of a countless number in New Orleans that had to
be won over. And all these places were filled. At different times
of the day, audiences entered whose tastes corresponded to their
work shifts.

The earliest evening crowd came from 3:00 to about 7:00 P.M.
after laboring construction, plaster, or painting. They needed
jukebox. At 5:30 arrived the few mildly successful men of commerce who needed peace. Those with more ambition cocktailed
in the business district. From then until 8:00 P.M. came wives

fetching their husbands or children their fathers. Also, families came in all together to take out oyster loaf sandwiches for dinner and sit while the parents drank one beer. They entertained themselves. Until 11:00 P.M. or later, 2:00 or 3:00 in the morning, visited people who were very lonely or out of ideas. They sought out others to excite them by new thoughts, words, or deeds.

O.C. and Aces provided the latter nourishment. She sang sad, slow, sweet blues songs. On no platform, she was directly ahead of them and level with their chairs. Some nights, her performance began as if she had simply arrived through the front door or returned from the bathroom, and rather than take a seat she began singing. For her casualness, the audience appreciated her even more.

Oceola proved to them that anyone could have a song down deep and with the right kind of spirit one could just open one's mouth and it would escape. It would fly out beautiful and melodious, grand and important. The singular feeling possessed by all that she captured was the soul of them.

Aces was counterpoint to her beauty. He was a small man full of wiry energy. That impelled him to fly, although in another direction from Oceola, as he tap-danced on floors, chairs, tables and made rhythms against the wall. "There's no stopping him," O.C. introduced at the end of her performance and the beginning of his.

But he was already stopped by the public. In those years, tap dancing was seen as a kind of plantation throwback, a degrading form that appealed to degenerates. So Aces' fate, actually, was to go nowhere and there he brought Oceola.

O.C. also sang some of the country songs learned from her father. When he was younger, and more joyful, he taught her to play guitar. In the swamps where she lived as the only child, Oceola listened to her voice—clear, light and youthful. It cut through the denseness of moss and waterlogged trees to create soft responses. Still, she learned modulation, pitch, and performance from hearing her own echoes.

When people gathered, as they did in those years, at the homes of friends on holidays, Oceola would sing to the room. Those faces were grateful to see her healthy on those few times a year, much less to enjoy her experience. In their enthusiasm, they encouraged her, "Oceola, people should hear you in New Orleans."

"Is nothing but sin in those cities," her father, who would eventually raise Joan to stay home, then discouraged Oceola. But she continued to practice and others said, "Don't waste your talents." She did not tell them to leave was forbidden.

Finally, she snuck off with a boy to New Orleans for a day on the pretense of going to fish. Her father paced from the time they should have been home, in the afternoon, to early the next morning when they returned.

Oceola did not lie. Her life would be wasted if she lived in the swamp. She had a talent, she argued. Few people still lived like they did in the swamp, she said.

It was true. Most of the people who gathered for holidays had moved, if not to the cities, to rural communities where they would be closer to other people. The old man refused. His house still served him well. The swamp was there before some people and would remain after.

And, although he did not say, he feared trying to live any place except where he was. In the swamp, he could hunt, fish, and for cash collect and sell moss. His existence did not involve streetcars and banks, telephones, automobiles, and the rush and excitement to use or own them. In the swamp, he had all he needed; that was enough. The part of his reasoning that he told Oceola was, "Enough." He said, "Enough," to her questions. Often, he shouted it.

Oceola left home feeling "enough" most applied to her existence. She had outlived her usefulness to him. If her father made do with the necessary, her desire to commit to something as frivolous as song was superfluous.

She was wrong. He was so lonely for her voice after Oceola left that his joy fell off him in pounds. The small animals he caught now resembled him in proportion. And then, when he set them on his dinner table, even they seemed too large for him to cut up and eat by himself. For a while, he thought he was dying. His only friend was the doctor who visited once a week. The doctor came around more to reassure and comfort the man than for physical reasons.

Oceola returned less than a year later. She brought Joan with her, proof Oceola was lonely too. But she had taken a woman's recourse and was too proud to let her father call it her sin. Her face was drawn tight with tension. Her body appeared aged. Her lips were too bright, and the skin around her eyes was too dark. The eyes themselves were dim. When she had left the swamp, her total appearance showed clear and lighthearted. When she returned weariness was all about her. She was weighted with this new life, the father observed. He asked her to stay and she did for a little while. But the time was too late; she could not remain in the dark and the silence.

She said when she handed the baby to the old man, "I hope you do better with her than me."

The Blue Peacock and its neighborhood was the site of her brief urban life before having the baby. Oceola was only seventeen. The boy who first brought her to New Orleans found her a room in a house close to his city relatives. But Oceola did not see him again after she refused to have sex.

"Come on, girl, grow up." He tried intimidation. He tried love. But Oceola knew better. She told him that. So finally, he tried force. She would have to listen because she was alone in the city and she knew only him. He miscalculated. She pulled out the hunting knife in her pocket.

It was about nine inches long with a blade that eased back just a little like a saber. It was capable of easily slicing a small animal from the gut to the throat.

"If you want to keep everything you got now, you leave me alone forever," Oceola advised. He listened. She did right, but after that she was even lonelier, with neither friend nor enemy.

In her single room near the back entrance of an old lady's house, Oceola passed the days playing guitar. She ate very little. The same sandwiches and hard meat went down day after day. That wasn't too bad; she was accustomed to a diet that offered little variety in a particular season.

She also knew how to amuse herself. But in the city was a different feeling to being alone, unlike in the swamp, where she took living company from the trees, water, and birds. Here was little in nature to communicate to her. And there were people all around her that she could not contact. That was the worst.

Loneliness was harder to control here when she heard daily the voices of others, yet they did not speak to her. She even saw them if she looked out of her window. Oceola could almost touch them. But she did not know them. So she felt they had nothing in common and no desire for her acquaintance.

A young man who saw her sitting outside on the porch took the initiative finally. Aces was the first person to take an interest in Oceola in New Orleans.

Aces got his name because he was a four-flusher, everyone knew. In fact, he ran out of neighborly people with whom to associate himself. He too was lonely for company of a good nature. He sought it out constantly, although when people opened their hearts to him, or their homes, he took advantage.

He sensed Oceola's purity. He practically smelled it from where he stood in the street. Her face was almost bright with innocence. All he said was "Hello" and her conversation gushed out.

He invited himself to her porch step that afternoon and then daily. By the time the old lady in the front of the house told Oceola that Aces was bad, she could not agree. He showed Oceola only his kind side, as he did with most new people. From her perspective, she never met anyone so concerned with her so sweetly.

He learned that she played guitar. He danced. "A match made in heaven." He found her soft spot. Her first job was through Aces at the Blue Peacock. She did not realize that because of her singing, he would rest more instead of dance and he collected more than a fair share of the paycheck.

She was just thrilled to get money for performance. She invited Aces one night for dinner. He stayed overnight, sealing himself to her. She got pregnant almost immediately.

As she grew big, he removed the embraces. She thought at first, maybe her want had increased. Or perhaps her memory was skewed from the too-clearheadedness of not drinking alcohol in the club as she did between sets, eating more, and going to the bathroom often. Did Aces care for her less? Sometimes she sat, observer to his affection. No, he did not massage her shoulders anymore, pass his hand down her back, kiss the part in her hair.

At the Blue Peacock she saw him treat other women. And she

believed half of what she saw, like the blues song said. But she believed all of what she heard, as it advised against.

Aces introduced her to the abortionist. Oceola was one month farther along than she told anyone. But she was less afraid of this lie than of Aces. Just as sweet as he was at first, now he was evil. He had no in-between.

Oceola never was in the company of a man except her father. Still Aces' threats did not seem right. They fought bitterly when she ran away from Irene Campland. She planned to leave after the baby was born. And she did. Back to the swamp. But she could not stay there. She had acquired a taste, however bad, for the outside. Perhaps the excitement itself served as her addiction or just the basic human desire to finish life in a different way than it had begun.

Her mistake the second time was to live as she had learned from Aces. He taught that men were out only to do women wrong. She found this to be true time after time. Soon time itself began to pass quickly between the men and also briefly with them as she searched for the right one.

In the French Quarter, her habit of promiscuity turned profitable easily. The career of prostitute started with Aces' training. When she worked at the Blue Peacock, she had sex with his friends for his pleasure. Then he forced her to, or he would beat her. Later she rationalized the money she got paid for the previous free use of herself.

Now she no longer sang.

If she was seventeen again, she still didn't know the best decision. The solitude of the swamp or the excitement of the city? The waste of her talent or the misuse of it?

And often she actually wished to see her daughter to tell her the pain of life and the need to escape from it. But what would Oceola recognize? The child would be completely changed. O.C. named her Blue, after the place where she worked and the color of sky that she first saw outside the swamp. If Oceola thought about it, she could almost picture Blue's face, floating like a song travels, becoming a ghostly presence over the grey hanging moss. Except for the tinge, Oceola's image was very close to her child's real appearance.

The doctor pushed the black-painted glass door to the Blue Peacock Room and saw that the sign did not lie. The club, transformed from an old liquor store by distorted drawings of blue cocktail glasses and pink elephants, was one cubical. Its proportions of length and width were equally small. The ceiling was not very high.

The room was dark, not unusual. But it smelled slightly fresher than other barrooms.

"Well, business," the bartender said absently out of surprise when the doctor entered. The bartender did not expect company lately, he said. As he explained to the doctor, the clientele now came mostly on Thursday and Friday. Most of them would finish their paycheck in that one night, or the majority of it. So he had few customers at other times.

The doctor had not yet sat. He strolled the room slowly, close to the walls. There hung photos of entertainers in the Blue Peacock's better days, the bartender said. He pointed out names, "Johnny Taylor, Ernie K-Do, Lee 'Ya-Ya' Dorsey." It was an opportunity for the doctor to ask, "You ever heard of O.C. and Aces?"

"You mean Aces and O.C.," the bartender corrected. "They had a day or two. Look over there."

As the doctor walked to the corner and leaned over one of the four or five blue formica-topped tables in the room, the bartender continued, "Everyone know he done her bad. I was here then. Long time ago. Don't seem like it 'cause I was here then. But I was just a child." The bartender laughed in a husky voice that brought phlegm to his throat that he spit in a coffee can. "I was here to see Miss O.C. herself. She was so beautiful and so sweet. And not much more than my age." The bartender threw his index finger harder in the doctor's direction, "See them, there?"

"No. I can't tell," said the doctor.

The bartender came out from behind the bar. He limped on the left. "From the war," he explained. He and the doctor exchanged cordial and tight-lipped smiles and dropped their eyes. "There she is. Look," the bartender was the first to recover. "She wouldn't have nothing to do with me. When I begged her. Before my stuff happened." The doctor and bartender glanced at the floor together. "When I was young and pretty myself, that Aces had her locked up. And when I come back," the bartender pulled the tail of a soiled white rag out of his waistband and dusted the black drugstore frame of the photo, "I was scared to even wish it. Like I was." He mumbled the last sentence. Then he grew loud, "That Aces, man. I hate him. I swear I hate him. I'm glad he's dead and I know what that means. But it wasn't my wish that killed him. I guess I don't wish it on nobody anyway. Was the horse took him out. You know, heroin."

The last part, that there would be no Aces to talk to, the doctor heard. Most of the rest, he half listened to. He stared intently at the small photo of a thin, slick-haired man and a young girl on his lap wearing a dress with a slit on the side opened up further to show the photographer most of her left leg.

Except for her hair bob and lips opened in a provocative smile, the face of O.C. was the same as of the girl, Joan, who now waited in the room in the French Quarter for word of whether her mother would provide a home.

The other resemblance the doctor hadn't expected. Joan's eyes that curved into almonds, even the slight bags below them, belonged to the man. Aces looked to be very much Joan's father, although that place on her birth certificate was blank.

"Dead, huh? His people around here bury him? Who?" the doctor asked.

"The city, far as I know, and ain't nobody to care." The bartender moved back behind the counter.

The doctor bought him a beer. "You know where Oceola is now? She's not dead, is she?"

"You know her? Is she all right?" the bartender responded. Realizing that he too was searching—asking a question while not realizing the question was directed at him, the bartender said, "Not since that last night, twelve, fifteen years ago? I couldn't look at her after that." The bartender leaned down and closer, "See I always wanted her. And, man, I needed it bad when I come back from the war, some love and affection. And me and O.C., we were—before I went, anyway—like joking friends. And I come back like I am and she say she don't mind. And we do it, and I think, 'God, let me marry her.' But you know what she say when I'm leaving up out the door, even saying 'Baby, thank you.' She say, 'Fifteen dollars.' I ask, 'What?' She say, 'Fifteen dollars for that. I give you a good deal.'"

The bartender drank out of his beer, put his hand up to his face, and balanced his elbow on the arm across his chest. He stood slack, all of him leaning now to the right. "I just couldn't keep up with her after that. I changed and she changed. Maybe they ain't no real difference because we both poor off. But there is. I feel there is."

The men were both silent for a long time. Both sipped beer and looked at anything in the room but the faces of each other. Neither wanted to turn the corner on sadness. That would be like staring at the attachment of skin chewed by the shells.

The doctor spoke first, "You think I could have that picture?" He pointed to O.C. and Aces against the wall. "Her daughter is looking for her. . . ."

The bartender cut in excitedly, "She had a child?"

"Here, give her this." The bartender reached to his back pocket and took out a very old wallet. Out of a broken and yellowed plastic sleeve, he took a photo of Oceola. She was young with a clear face and a smile that showed no lipstick and much more sincerity. On the back was written in a shaky hand with fountain pen, "To George. From O.C." The bartender said, "Oh. I wrote that in the war."

The doctor looked at the picture in his palm. She was almost a different person than the one on Aces' lap.

"Give her this picture, not the other one. Tell her you found it or something. Don't tell her about Aces. That was a bad time," the bartender said.

"I don't know." The doctor started to hand the photo back.

"Keep it, please."

The doctor agreed slowly to that.

"Maybe, in a few years," the bartender stammered, "if you don't find her mother, you could tell the child—what's her name? . . ."

"Joan," the doctor said.

"Maybe in the future, you could tell her to look up George, if she need to. Not now. Now you speak for me."

The doctor nodded yes and went to the door after placing the photo in his own wallet. He thanked the bartender.

"If you see O.C., tell her George say, 'How you doing?'" the bartender asked.

"You know, that could have been my baby," he said as the doctor pulled open the door. They both nodded agreement and looked in their different directions.

The photo in the doctor's pocket had life of its own. Energy radiated from it, making him feel touched and tense. All the way back to the French Quarter apartment, the doctor tried to decide whether to show the picture to Joan now or to wait until they found her mother.

He did not want to get the girl's hopes too high. But the photo felt as if it wanted to be seen. The doctor was compelled to pull it out of his pocket again during the cab ride. The driver asked if the doctor came from out of town and whether he wanted a "date." The driver's talk was distracting. Finally, the doctor asked, "Please be quiet."

"You some kind of priest?" the cabdriver said. The doctor ignored him. Oceola's face showed so much hope. She could have picked any man before Joan was born. Perhaps she remained in New Orleans to find someone again. And not having found anyone, she stayed away. Or maybe she did find a man and she lived with him now, and with the children they made.

From the photo, he could see Oceola was once as childlike as Joan.

It must have been very hard for them both not to grow up around others. In his childhood home were so many brothers and sisters that worldly wisdom increased to the youngest, as it was passed down. But Joan was barely socialized. When they went to a restaurant in New Orleans, Joan picked up the meat with her fingers and broke it with her teeth. She chewed roughly, the way the doctor imagined Eskimos ate blubber. But even they, far in the North, had community in these manners.

Joan's mother was probably equally out of place when she arrived in New Orleans. The doctor saw from her picture, she vainly tried to be a sophisticate. She wore a small sequined hat like a soup bowl placed askew on her head. Net gushed out from the top like a fountain, the veil going up hopefully but then cascading.

Joan got the photo from the doctor as soon as he walked in the door. She guessed he had found something. Then she ran into her room to examine the picture alone. Joan did not turn on the light to the bedroom. She could see clearly enough because in the swamp she relied most times on lamps. Plus, she felt more comfortable without the buzzing and spitting of manmade illumination. Instead, Joan went to the window and pulled the long drapes aside so she could see by the moon.

But the streetlights overcame the cosmos. The moon was apparent but not usable. So Joan pretended the conditions were natural under which she first saw her mother.

The face was like Joan's in the oval shape of the bones and innocence of the smooth skin. But the eyes were almost tearful in their pretended joy. The mouth smiled. But there was tension across the top of the parted lips. Joan could see that her mother tried to please and was fearful of not succeeding.

Joan wept when she saw it. This is the way she imagined her mother. Joan thought her mother was weak. Her death, as she was in Joan's mind for many years, was proof of Joan's mother's inability to survive. And if her mother was alive, Joan imagined protection was still needed. Joan would say, "Mother, come home to the swamp where it is more peaceful."

"Mother, come home," she whispered now to the picture. She held the photo close to her face and stared at it until she could imagine the mouth spoke. "I miss you, Joan," the picture said. "I would do anything to be with you."

Joan folded her arms so that the picture lay close to her heart. Then she fell asleep. The doctor came into the room later and saw the girl on the floor next to the window, leaned against the wall. But he did not want to startle her. She had already had one shock. Plus, he did not want to spoil the movement in her dreams.

In them, Joan spoke with Oceola on the porch of the house in the swamp. The mother said, "Joan, I did not intend to leave you. I just got lost on the way home. I want you again."

"It's OK, Mother," Joan replied. "I knew you hadn't deserted me. It was grandfather's fault."

Joan began to feel very angry in her dream. She looked for her grandfather all through the house. But he would not come to her call and she heard a splash in the water off the side porch. She got there too late, only to see her grandfather's heels and then toes slipping into the swamp, as if in a dive. That made Joan madder. And she began to hear herself cry loudly, "I want ma mére. Where is she?" But instead of her mother the school-teacher appeared. "In New Orleans," she said. Joan heard her, although she did not listen. Instead, she wept.

Joan awoke feeling bad. The room was very dark. She re-membered the apartment in the French Quarter. She thought, how would the Bible advise her in this situation? "Seek to find," immediately came to Joan.

Joan stepped to the balcony and found the drainpipe nearby. She slipped down to the sidewalk. And when the doctor knocked on the door the next time, Joan did not answer.

There were no girls Joan's age walking through the French Quarter streets in the dark. There were men and women hold-ing onto each other in most obvious ways. Many of them seemed mismatched, Joan could tell by their fashions. She no-ticed that one of the couple wore very bright clothes while the other had on dark colors. Pushed up against each other in door-ways or heaped together in cars, they first appeared to Joan like sparrows nesting with bluejays.

Then Joan understood that their activities were just as pri-vate. Shocked, she rushed in the direction of noise. On Bourbon Street, the doorways blasted more sound than Joan's ears could stand. The reverberations of trumpets, drums, and loud off-key singers slipped right through her ears into her brain. She left that street where men called to her often and when she turned around to answer them, made what appeared to be mean signals with their mouths and their hands. Joan hurried on, getting far-ther to the back of Esplanade and near the French Quarter, feel-ing sadder and nearer somehow to her mother.

Actually, Oceola was near the vegetable carts in a doorway waiting for someone to respond. Her presence was felt by Joan as a feeling of overwhelming sorrow and melancholy. When Joan walked past the group of men lingering and making their minds up not far from her mother, she did not stop as they asked for her and then threatened. But she rushed away in tears and confusion.

She had walked in a circle. She discovered nothing she

wanted. Joan rang the bell of the apartment building to be let in. The doctor answered, "You can't do this running away no more."

They went upstairs to talk. "I'm shamed how you acting," the doctor said to her. "You got to think and act like an adult now. If you didn't find your mother, what, huh?"

"That's not possible," Joan's pride now lied to cover the realization she made on the streets. New Orleans was big and loud and hard. She might not find her mother among all these people. She tried hard to picture herself and her mother happy in New Orleans. But instead, she saw the day she sat on the porch feeling bad because her grandfather had said Joan had no mother alive. It was the day he and the schoolteacher argued. When her grandfather took her home, he came out to the front porch to comfort Joan.

She remembered pushing him. "I want ma mére," she said.

"What about me?" Joan remembered he looked hurt.

"You are a man," she said.

Then he put an old rag over his head and tied a knot under the chin. He began talking to Joan in a squeaking high voice. She could not help but begin laughing.

Her grandfather then made her happy just as the doctor was trying to now. They wanted to give of themselves to satisfy her emptiness. But they could not fill it. Her mother was special, Joan knew, although they had never met. Just that she bore Joan showed a connection the men would never understand.

Her mother gave life to Joan for a good reason, she felt. Why else would a woman have a child? Joan remembered once when her grandfather left the supply store first, the lady behind the counter offered a package of roots. "Make tea out of these if you ever need them. Then you won't have a baby," she said.

Why would a woman not want a baby, Joan wondered. And that time she said, "The babies are nice. They small and they soft. But me, I can't have one no way."

"The babies is trouble. You never heard of getting in trouble? Child, you too innocent." The store woman pushed the package of roots into Joan's hand, "for when you will need them."

Joan kept the roots for a very long time. She put them near her bed under the Bible in case they were bad magic and she needed protection from hell. Then one time, a boy at the school pushed Joan into the closet and kissed her. She was upset and knew then she would get pregnant. She thought about telling her grandfather, and how if she told him about the boy, he would take her away from school. Joan liked school. She wanted to go there as long as possible to read and then maybe to study with the nuns, as her teacher once suggested to her. The kiss would prevent her unless she did something about it. Joan decided to take the roots. If the kiss got her pregnant, that would rid it, make it go backwards, away. She prayed that the kiss would return out of her. It did, like vomit.

Joan was so sick her stomach ached for days. But she did not tell her grandfather or the doctor when he came what had happened.

But while she was ill and laying in some delusions, she forgot who she was. She dreamed that she was her mother, advising her grandfather, "Don't tell Joan who I am. Don't tell her they kissed me until I died." Joan did not tell her grandfather about this dream. And she came to understand the need for having a secret. Her mother had one too. Joan wasn't sure what the secret was. But it had to do with kissing, and babies and dying. And men could not feel about it the same way as women.

Joan rose at about six the next morning in the French Quarter apartment. The doctor had talked to her the previous night about not running away anymore, growing up and starting a new life. Joan understood that he did not want her to return alone to the swamp. He wanted her to live with him or go work for the nuns. He said they could still try to find her mother.

Joan stood on the balcony looking at New Orleans beginning to rise. The sun was not visible as she looked toward the river. But she already felt the morning heat. Below Joan on the balcony, a group of women walked and talked loudly. Their laughs sounded false, coming out of fatigue and despondency. One of them was a redhead. Joan immediately felt the same excitement as when she received the photo. She felt her mother among them.

Joan raced out of her bedroom, through the living room where Claudia and the doctor sat. She ran down the steps of the building and into the street. The first call she could think of was a mockingbird whistle, a high screeching imitation of cats.

Oceola heard the sound behind her. It was familiar. But she couldn't place it.

The doctor ran right after Joan into the streets. He yelled, "Stop."

Oceola Leontine, having lived the last eighteen years with an immediate response to that word from a man, began running. But before she ran she noticed the girl coming after her. Oceola thought, "What a shame, a kid that young in the trade." She was just about that age and probably not as pretty when she began, Oceola considered. She was running, but slower than the other women. Her night had been uneventful, unprofitable, and discouraging. Oceola wished she was as young as that girl running away from the man. She was not. Too many years had passed. She was old and broke down, and who knew how she would become?

The girl was beginning to gain on Oceola. She was crying, whistling loud like mockingbirds. She must be crazy, Oceola thought. That man might be trying to put her away. But the sounds were so familiar to Oceola they made her feel crazy and confused too.

"Hurry up. Get out of here, fool." The women ahead of Oceola told her to catch up. Instead, she stopped and leaned into her boot. She pulled out her long blade knife. She would give it to the child. If the girl was crazy, she could destroy the man. No big loss. If she needed only to get away from him, the knife was her diversion.

Oceola left the blade on the ground where it glimmered a streak of light back to the sun. Oceola ran, then stood on the corner to watch. The girl ran by the blade. But the man picked it up.

After looking at the blade in his hands, and hesitating, the man finally brought his arm back and threw it. He was a poor aim. But it still landed near O.C. He had tried to get her.

At the same time, the girl arrived. "You my mother?"

"God." Oceola took Joan's hand. They ran down the street out of the French Quarter and into the safety of her apartment.

The doctor stood in the sunlit street, now angered and upset by his decision. He had tried all along to save this girl's life, to do right by her and all of her kind. Hadn't he always ministered to those who had nothing and sympathized with their hopeless situations? But Joan deserted him just as he tried to help. That was her choice, he conceded. But the means he had chosen, that's what upset him. He was not a man to believe in the sword. Yet such was his decision if that innocent girl ran straight into the arms of harm. He would hurt whomever stood in his way to protect her. Maybe a good man did have to use violence for a better outcome. Or maybe each person had a violence in them that arose when faced with a situation they could not control. He had succumbed to his baser emotion.

Joan and Oceola Leontine, out of breath, rested in her living room on the old brocade couch. The daughter leaned back and looked around the room. Damask and aged curtains and furniture displayed an affinity for darkness in this first part of the house that did not fit with the outside Oceola.

Oceola's red hair, heavy makeup, and bright orange dress were colored so obviously to be out of place here where her walls, floors, and even decorations were in shades of deep blue, green, and grey. Additionally, an aquarium gave the room an odd light. The fish moved in front of the fluorescence like three-dimensional shadows.

Oceola rose and opened the curtains so that the room changed and so did she in it. The straight rays of sunlight coming in the length of the window seemed to throw into the house a cast of brightness almost artificial in its intensity. And only the fronts of the furniture and even Oceola herself were lit. The backs remained in shadow as if everything had a covered and undiscoverable side. The light on her mother, Joan thought, made a mask of her face—painted bright in the front and smiling with tension—over the true depth of her thoughts.

Joan wordlessly watched her mother, now energetically moving around the room. She appeared to be nervous with Joan staring.

"I knew I would find you. Granddaddy's dead," Joan said.

"Oh. I expected that happen some time," Oceola replied.

"Did you miss me?" Joan asked.

"As much as I knew of you I missed." Oceola did not look into Joan's eyes.

"I didn't know that you were around. So I guess I didn't miss you much either," Joan reflected her mother's statement. For Joan the words were said in truth.

Oceola, however, had lied. She knew her daughter existed and she could have visited Joan with her grandfather. Because of that Oceola did miss Joan and the opportunity of having a child. She knew that and she felt guilty. But she could not say it now, just as in the past she could do nothing about her own loneliness that kept her away from the people she loved.

As Joan continued to stare, Oceola moved to the record player. "This your first time to New Orleans?" Oceola fell back on her repertoire of meaningless statements, with which she was more confident and familiar.

"Yes. Didn't you want a daughter?" Joan continued with questions.

"I wanted you to be better than me."

"The fruit drops not far from the tree." Joan remembered her Bible, which had explained her mother's behavior while Joan was young and wondering.

"Oh. You don't know." Oceola began to speak of a life her daughter never discovered in her religious reading. Oceola spoke frankly, sparing no details about the life of a prostitute: Johns, living outside of the law, deaths, drugs, alcoholism in women. She told her daughter about selling the body and how the product cheapens with age. Oceola offered her life with candor as she had learned to speak to the women and men of the street. But this time, she told her story with sadness, since she finally had someone to hear her problems. In fact, Oceola was so overwhelmed by her own continuing trouble that she did not notice the face of her daughter.

The stories were wasted on Joan, who could not appreciate her mother's cleverness and skill as Oceola described her talent for staying alive. Her mother's behavior went strictly against the codes Joan learned from the Bible. Joan tried to understand and reminded herself that this was her mother. She should listen as the Lord would to sinners.

For her part, Oceola assumed her daughter already had similar experiences because of the man chasing Joan. Oceola had been out in the street so long she could not imagine the mentality of a virgin.

So Oceola just unburdened herself. She made herself a drink as she talked. The art of listening, so practiced by women in Oceola's profession, was also the job of listening. So on her own time and finally with someone to care, Oceola paid no attention to her audience.

When Oceola so easily said she had expected hell for considering the abortion and was happy to see her daughter alive, Joan fell sad, finally understanding her mother in a way her grandfather could never have explained.

Oceola had said, "See, I ran out of that place so fast. Shoot. I was a sight then. I didn't know nothing. But I knew enough that that old lady could have killed me with what she was planning. And Aces knew too. And you think he would have cared. Who? Honey, that man was shit. It's good he's dead and you never met him. Well, I got out all right. And when the baby was born, I said, I can't take care of that thing here in New Orleans."

Oceola had slipped. She had told the story so often. She had not made the connection between the "thing" and her daughter sitting in front of her. But Joan had. And then she decided that she was better off without a mother than with one like this.

As Oceola talked rapidly, still moving often from chair to record player to liquor cabinet, Joan rose slowly and deliberately.

"Could I have your address, so I can write you?"

"Where you going? We just getting to know each other. Baby, don't go back to no bad man. They not worth anything," Oceola said.

"Mama, Oceola. I'm just doing the best for myself." Joan walked toward the door, ready to memorize the numbers in case she ever wanted to return. But right then, she had to leave. She was not a thing. She was Joan. She was not city clever. But she was wise and alive. She did not feel she should have been thrown out because she disturbed Oceola's life either before she was born or after. Oceola had still not realized that.

"How could you kill me before I was born?" Joan asked.

"Baby, sit down. But I didn't. And I didn't know it was you

to come out. You were nothing to me then. I did not even see you."

"And you haven't seen me since." Joan opened the door for herself.

"Child, don't go now. I need to have you around now that I know you're alive."

"I can leave, Oceola, now that I know you."

Joan stepped out the front door of the apartment in the Marigny into the sunlight. Her mother stood in the frame. She was slightly drunk from drinking and talking so fast. Joan looked around and waved from the sidewalk. But Oceola was distracted by something in her living room and did not see Joan turn back before walking away.

Joan felt older and grown. No matter what the doctor said, she was going to live again in the swamp. Joan was ready to take care of herself. She did not need her childish imagination anymore. She had seen the reality of her mother and could give her up.

Her mother had given Joan to her grandfather because for Oceola that was the best choice, Joan considered. Now she was better alone. Becoming a woman meant saving oneself, Joan suddenly realized, and maybe, if possible, another person.

Before she left, Joan had told Oceola, "If you get tired of money and men using you like you say, you could do different."

When Joan found her way back to the French Quarter apartment, the doctor and Claudia were waiting. Hearing her story, they decided to return to the country. The doctor agreed to let Joan go back to the swamp after he made some arrangements for her to be looked after and work for the supply store woman. Joan spent a few weeks in the doctor's house getting prepared to go home.

When Joan got in her pirogue, she didn't want anyone but the dog to return with her to the house. She paddled through the swamp, now smelling its decay compared to the open air outside. But she felt comfortable. The swamp showed little passage of time and none but the most dramatic of changes. But she was accustomed to it and she had more peace here than any place else.

Joan greeted in tears the house where her grandfather died. She tied her boat up to the side of the porch and climbed the stairs. She went to the screen to undo the zipper of bent nails. But it was already open. The dog ran in ahead. Joan came in more slowly, wondering what she would find after so many weeks. Was her grandfather back alive?

Oceola Leontine stood waiting for her daughter. "I will try," she said. "This is better for both of us." Oceola opened her arms and Joan fell into them like a child and also finally a woman comforted.